DORUNTINE

also by Ismail Kadare
Chronicle in Stone

DORUNTINE

Ismail Kadare

*Translated from the French
of Jusuf Vrioni by*
Jon Rothschild

**SAQI
BOOKS**

© 1986, Librairie Arthème Fayard

All rights reserved.

Translation © 1988, Jon Rothschild

This edition first published 1988.
Saqi Books, 26 Westbourne Grove, London W2 5RH.

British Library Cataloguing in Publication Data:
Kadaré, Ismaïl
Doruntine.
I. Title
891'.9913[F]   PG9621.K3
ISBN 0-86356-171-3

Printed in the United States of America.

DORUNTINE

CHAPTER ONE

*S*tres was still in bed when he heard the knocking at the door. He was tempted to bury his head in the pillow to blot out the noise, but the sound came again, louder this time. Who the Devil would pound on my door before daybreak, he grumbled, throwing off the covers. He was on his way down the stairs when he heard the hammering for the third time, but now the rhythm of the metal knocker told him who it was. He slid back the bolt and opened the door. There was no need to say, "And what possesses you to wake me before dawn," for the look on his face and his bleary eyes conveyed the message well enough.

"Something's happened," his deputy hastened to say.

Stres stared at him skeptically, as if to say, And it better be good to justify a visit at this ungodly hour. But he was well aware that his aide rarely blundered. Indeed, whenever he had been moved to rebuke him, he had found himself compelled to hold his tongue. Still, he would have been delighted had his deputy been in the wrong this time, so that he could work off his ill humor on him.

"So?" he repeated.

The deputy glanced at his chief's eyes for an instant, then stepped back and spoke:

"The dowager Vranaj and her daughter, Doruntine, who arrived last night under very mysterious circumstances, both lie dying."

"Doruntine?" said Stres, dumbfounded. "How can it be?"

His deputy heaved a sigh of relief: he had been right to pound on the door.

"How can it be?" Stres said again, rubbing his eyes as if to wipe away the last trace of sleep. And in fact he had slept badly. No first night home after a two-week mission had ever been so trying. One long nightmare. "How can it be?" he asked for the third time. Doruntine had married into a family that lived so far from her own that she hadn't been able to come back even when her family was in mourning.

"How, indeed," said the deputy. "As I said, the circumstances of her return are most mysterious."

"And?"

"Well, both mother and daughter have taken to their beds and lie dying."

"Strange! Do you think there's been foul play?"

The deputy shook his head. "I think not. It looks more like the effect of some dreadful shock."

"Have you seen them?"

"Yes. They're both delirious, or close to it. The mother keeps asking, 'Who brought you back, daughter?' And the daughter keeps saying, 'My brother Constantine.'"

"Constantine? But he died three years ago, he and all his brothers. . . ."

"According to the neighbor women now gathered at the bedside, that is just what the mother told her. But the girl insists that she arrived with him last night, just after midnight."

"How odd," said Stres, all the while thinking, "Horrible."

They stared at each other in silence until Stres, shivering, remembered that he was not dressed.

"Wait for me," he said, and went back in.

From inside came his wife's drowsy "What is it?" and the inaudible words of his reply. Soon he came out again, wearing the regional captain's uniform that made him look even taller and thinner.

"Let's go see them," he said.

They set out in silence. A handful of white rose petals fallen at someone's door seemed to remind Stres of a brief scene from the dream that had slipped so strangely into his fitful sleep.

"Quite extraordinary," he said.

"Almost incredible," replied his deputy, upping the ante.

"To tell you the truth, at first I was tempted not to believe it."

"So I noticed. In fact it isn't believable. It's a real mystery."

"Worse than that," Stres said. "The more I think about it, the more inconceivable it seems."

"The main thing is to find out how Doruntine got back," said the deputy.

"What?"

"The case will be solved if we can find out who accompanied her, or rather, if we can uncover the circumstances of her arrival."

"Who accompanied her," Stres repeated. "Yes, who and how. Obviously she is not telling the truth."

"I asked her three times how she got here, but she offered no explanation. She was hiding something."

"Did she know that all her brothers, including Constantine, were dead?" Stres asked.

"I don't know. I don't think so."

"It's possible she didn't know," Stres said. "She married so far away that she has never once come home since her wedding day. This is the first time so far as I know."

"She didn't come back even when her nine brothers died, which seems proof enough that she was utterly unaware of the calamity," said the deputy. "The dowager complained often enough that her daughter was not at her side during those days of grief."

"The forests of Bohemia lie at least two weeks' journey from here, if not more," Stres observed.

"Yes, if not more," repeated his deputy. "Almost the heart of Europe."

As they walked Stres noticed more white rose petals strewn along the path, as if some invisible hand had scattered them during the night.

"In any event, someone must have come with her," he said.

"Yes, but who? Her mother can't possibly believe that her daughter returned with a dead man, any more than we can."

"But why would she conceal who she came back with?"

"I can't explain it. It's all very puzzling."

Once again they walked in silence. The autumn air was cold. Some cawing crows flew low. Stres watched their flight for a moment.

"It's going to rain," he said. "The crows caw like that because their ears hurt when a storm is coming."

His deputy looked off in the same direction, but said nothing.

"Earlier you mentioned something about a shock that might have brought the two women to their deathbed," Stres said.

"Well, it was certainly caused by some very powerful emotion." He avoided the word *terrible,* for his chief had commented that he tended to use it in any and all circumstances. "Since neither woman shows any mark of violence, their sudden collapse must surely have been caused by some kind of shock."

"Do you think the mother suddenly discovered something terrible?" Stres asked.

His deputy stared at him. He can use words as he pleases, he thought, but if others do he stuffs those words down their throat.

"The mother?" he said. "I rather suspect that they both suddenly discovered something terrible, as you put it. At the same time."

As they continued to speculate about the shock mother and daughter had presumably inflicted on each other (both Stres and his deputy, warped by professional habit, increasingly tended to turns of phrase better suited to an investigative report), they mentally reconstructed, more or less, the scene that must have unfolded in the middle of the night. Knocks had sounded at the door of the old house at an unusual hour, and when the old lady called out—as she must have—"Who's there?"—a voice from outside would have answered, "It's me, Doruntine." Before opening the door, the old woman, upset by the sudden knocking and convinced that it could not have been her daughter's voice, must have asked, to ease her doubt, "Who brought you back?" Let us not forget that for three years she had been waiting in vain for her daughter's arrival, desperate for some consolation in her grief. From outside, Doruntine answers, "My brother Constantine brought me back." And the old woman receives the first shock. Perhaps, even shaken as she was, she found the strength to reply: "What are you talking about? Constantine and his brothers have been in their graves for three years." Now it is Doruntine's turn to be stricken. If she really believes that it was her brother Constantine who brought her back, then the shock is twofold: finding out that Constantine and her other brothers are dead and realizing at the same time that she has been traveling with a ghost. The old woman then summons up the strength to open the door, hoping against hope that she has misunderstood the young woman's words, or that she has been hearing voices, or that it is not Doruntine at the door after all. Perhaps Doruntine, standing there outside, also hopes she has misunderstood. But when the door swings open, both repeat what they have just said, dealing each other the fatal blow.

"No," said Stres. "None of that makes much sense either."

"That's just what I think," said his deputy. "But one thing is certain: something must have happened between them for the two women to be in such a state."

"Something happened between them," Stres repeated. "Of course something happened, but what? A terrifying tale from the girl, a terrifying revelation for the mother. Or else. . . ."

"There's the house," said the deputy. "Maybe we can find out something."

The great building could be seen in the distance, dismal, at the far end of a flat expanse. The wet ground was strewn with dead leaves all the way to the house, which had once been one of the grandest and most imposing of the principality, but which now had an air of mourning and desolation. Most of the shutters on the upper floors were closed, the eaves were damaged in places, and the grounds before the entrance, with their ancient, drooping, mossy trees, seemed desolate.

Stres recalled the burial of the nine Vranaj brothers three years before. There had been one tragedy after another, each more painful than the last, to the point that only by going mad could one erase the memory. But no generation could recall such a catastrophe: nine coffins for nine young men of a single household in just one week. It had happened five weeks after the grand wedding of the family's only daughter, Doruntine. The principality had been attacked without warning by a Norman army, and all nine brothers had gone off to war. It had often happened that several brothers of a single household went to fight in far more bloody conflicts, but never had more than half of them fallen in combat. This time, however, there was something very special about the enemy army: it was afflicted with plague, and most of those who took part in the fighting died one way or another, victors and vanquished alike, some in combat, others after the battle. Many a household had two, three, even four deaths to mourn, but only the Vranaj mourned for nine. No one could recall a more impressive funeral. All the counts and barons of the principality attended, even the prince himself, and dignitaries of neighboring principalities came as well.

Stres remembered it all quite clearly, most of all the words on everyone's lips at the time: how the mother, in those days of grief, did not have her only daughter, Doruntine, at her side. But Doruntine alone had not been told about the disaster.

Stres sighed. How quickly those three years had passed! The great double doors, worm-eaten in places, stood ajar. Walking ahead of his deputy, he crossed the courtyard and entered the house, from which he could hear vague murmuring. Two or three women, not young, apparently neighbors, examined the two new arrivals curiously.

"Where are they?" Stres asked.

One of the women nodded toward a door. Stres, followed by his deputy, walked into a vast, dimly lit room where his eyes were immediately drawn to two large beds set in opposite corners. Alongside each of these stood a woman, staring straight ahead. The icons on the walls, the two great copper candelabra above the fireplace, long unused, cast flickers of light through the atmosphere of gloom. One of the women turned her head toward them. Stres stopped for a moment, then motioned her to approach.

"Which is the mother's bed?" he asked softly.

The woman pointed to one of the beds.

"Leave us alone for a moment," Stres said.

The woman opened her mouth, doubtless to oppose him, but her gaze fell on Stres's uniform and she was silent. She walked over to her companion, who was very old, and both women went out without a word.

Walking carefully so as to make no noise, Stres approached the bed where the old woman lay, her head in the folds of a white bonnet.

"My Lady," he whispered, "Lady Mother"—for so had she been called since the death of her sons. "It's me, Stres, do you know me?"

She opened her eyes. They seemed glazed with

grief and terror. He withstood her gaze for a moment and then murmured, leaning a little nearer the white pillow, "How do you feel, Lady Mother?"

Her expression was unreadable.

"Doruntine came back last night, didn't she?" Stres asked.

The woman looked up from her bed, her eyes saying "yes." Her gaze then settled on Stres as though asking him some question. Stres stood there for a moment, hesitant.

"How did it happen?" he asked very softly. "Who brought her back?"

The old woman covered her eyes with one hand, then her head moved in a way that told him she had lost consciousness. Stres took her hand and found her pulse with difficulty. Her heart was still beating.

"Call one of the women," Stres said quietly to his deputy.

His aide left and soon returned with one of the women who had just left the room. Stres let go of the old woman's hand and, with the same silent steps, walked to the bed where Doruntine lay. He could see her blond hair on the pillow. He felt a wrench at his heart, but the sensation had nothing to do with what was happening now. A distant wrench, it went back to that wedding three years before. On that day, as she rode off on the customary white horse in the cavalcade of relatives and friends of the bride, his heart was suddenly so heavy that he wondered what had come over him. Everyone looked sad, not only Doruntine's mother and brother, but all her relatives, for she was the first girl of the country to marry so far away. But Stres's sorrow was quite special. As she rode off, he realized all at once that the feeling he had had for her had been love. But it was a love without shape, a love which had never condensed, for he himself had gently prevented it. It was like the morning dew that appears for the first few minutes after sunrise, only to vanish during the other hours of day and night. The only moment when that bluish fog had nearly condensed, had tried to form itself into a cloud, was when she left. But it had been no more than an instant, quickly forgotten.

Stres stood at Doruntine's bed, looking steadily into her face. She was as beautiful as ever, perhaps even more beautiful, with those lips that seemed somehow full and light at the same time.

"Doruntine," he said in a very soft voice.

She opened her eyes. Deep within them he sensed a void that nothing could fill. He tried to smile at her.

"Doruntine," he said again. "Welcome home."

She stared at him.

"How do you feel?" he said slowly, carefully, and unconsciously he took her hand. She was burning hot. "Doruntine," he said again, more gently, "you came last night after midnight, didn't you?"

Her eyes answered "yes." He would rather have put off asking the question that troubled him, but it rose up of itself.

"Who brought you back?"

The young woman's eyes stared steadily back at his own.

"Doruntine," he asked again, "who brought you back?"

Still she stared at him with those eyes in whose depths gaped a desperate void.

"You told your mother that it was your brother Constantine, didn't you?"

Again her look assented. Stres searched her eyes for some sign of madness, but could read nothing in their emptiness.

"I think you must have heard that Constantine left this world three years ago," he said in the same faint voice. He felt tears well up within him before they suddenly filled her eyes. But hers were tears unlike any others, half-visible, half-impalpable. Her face, bathed by those tears, seemed even more remote. What's happening to me? her eyes seemed to say. Why don't you believe me?

He turned slowly to his deputy and to the other woman standing near the mother's bed and motioned to them to leave. Then he leaned toward the young woman again and stroked her hand.

"How did you get here, Doruntine? How did

you manage that long journey?"

It seemed to him that something strained to fill those immeasurably enlarged eyes.

Stres left an hour later. He looked pale, and without turning his head or speaking a word to anyone, he made his way to the door. His deputy, following behind, was tempted several times to ask whether Doruntine had said anything new, but he did not dare.

As they passed the church, Stres seemed about to enter the cemetery, but changed his mind at the last minute.

His deputy could feel the glances of curious onlookers as they walked along.

"It's not an easy case," Stres said without looking at his deputy. "I expect there will be quite a lot of talk about it. Just to anticipate any eventuality, I think we would do well to send a report to the Prince's chancellery."

I believe it useful to bring to your attention events that occurred at dawn on this October eleventh in the noble house of Vranaj and whose consequences may be unpredictable.

On the morning of October 11, Lady Vranaj, who as everyone knows has been living alone since the death of her nine sons on the battlefield, was found in a state of profound distress, along with her daughter, Doruntine, who, by her own account, had arrived the night before, accompanied by her brother Constantine, who died three years ago when her other brothers died.

Having repaired to the site and tried to speak with the two unfortunate women, I concluded that neither showed any sign of mental irresponsibility, though what they now claim, whether directly or indirectly, is completely baffling and incredible. It is as well to note at this point that they had given each other this shock, the daughter by telling her mother that she had been brought home by her brother Constantine, the mother by informing her daughter that Constantine, with all her brothers, had long since departed this world.

I tried to discuss the matter with Doruntine, and what I managed to glean from her, in her distress, may be summarized more or less as follows:

One night not long ago (she does not recall the exact date), in the small city of central Europe in which she had been living with her husband since her marriage, she was told that a traveler was asking for her. On going out, she saw the horseman who had just arrived and who seemed to her to be Constantine, although the dust of the long journey had rendered him almost unrecognizable. But when the traveler, still in the saddle, said that he was indeed Constantine, and that he had come to take her to her mother as he had promised before her marriage, she was reassured. (Here we must recall the stir caused at the time by Doruntine's engagement to a man from a land so far away, the opposition of the other brothers and especially the mother, who did not want to send her daughter so far off, Constantine's insistence that the marriage take place, and finally his solemn promise, his *bessa,* that he would bring her back himself whenever their mother yearned for her daughter's company.)

Doruntine confided to me that her brother's behavior seemed rather strange, since he did not get off his horse and refused to go into the house. He insisted on taking her away as soon as possible, and when she asked him why she had to leave in such haste—for if the occasion was one of joy, she would don a holiday dress, and if it was one of sorrow, she would wear her mourning clothes—he said, with no further explanation, "Come as you are." His behavior was scarcely natural; moreover, it was contrary to all the rules of courtesy. But since she had been consumed with yearning for her family for these three years ("I lived in the most awful solitude," she says), she did not hesitate, wrote a note to her husband, and allowed her brother to lift her up behind him.

She also told me that it had been a long journey, though she was unable to say exactly how long. She says that all she remembers is an endless night, with myriad stars streaming across the sky, but this vision may have been suggested by an endless ride broken by longer or shorter intervals of sleep. It is interesting to note that she does not recall having traveled by day. She may have formed this impression either because she dozed or slept in the saddle all day, so that she no longer remembers the daylight at all, or because she and her escort retired at dawn and went to sleep, awaiting nightfall to continue their journey. Were this to prove correct, it would suggest that the rider wished to travel only by night. In Doruntine's mind, exhausted as she was (not to mention her emotional state), the ten or fifteen nights of the trip (for that is generally how long it takes to travel here from Bohemia) may have blended into a single long—indeed endless—nocturnal ride.

On the way, pressed against the horseman as she was, she noticed quite unmistakably that his hair was not just dusty, but covered with mud that was barely dry, and that his body smelled of sodden earth. Two or three times she questioned him about it. He answered that he had been caught in the rain several times on his way there and that the dust on his body and in his hair, thus moistened, had turned to clots of mud.

When, towards midnight of October eleventh, Doruntine and the unknown man (for let us so designate the man the young woman took to be her brother) finally approached the residence of the Lady Mother, he reined in his horse and told his companion to dismount and go to the house, for he had something to do at the church. Without waiting for an answer, he rode toward the church and the cemetery, while she ran to the house and knocked at the door. The old woman asked who was there, and then the few words exchanged between mother and daughter—the latter having said that it was she and that she had come with Constantine, the former replying that Constantine was three years dead—gave to both the shock that felled them.

This affair, which one is bound to admit is most puzzling, may be explained in one of two ways: either someone, for some reason, deceived Doruntine, posing as her brother with the express purpose of bringing her back, or Doruntine herself, for some unknown reason, has not told the truth and has concealed the manner of her return or the identity of the person who brought her back.

I thought it necessary to make a relatively detailed report about these events because they concern one of the noblest families in the principality and because they are of a kind that might seriously trouble people's minds.

Captain Stres

After initialing his report, Stres sat staring absently at his slanting handwriting. Two or three times he picked up his pen and was tempted to lean over the sheets of paper to amend, recast, or perhaps correct some passage, but each time he was about to put pen to paper his hand froze, and in the end he left his text unaltered.

He got up slowly, put the letter into an envelope, sealed it, and called for a messenger. When the man had gone, Stres stood for a long moment looking out the window, feeling his headache worsen. A crowd of theories jostled one another to enter his head as if through a narrow door. He rubbed his forehead as though to stem the flood. Why would an unknown traveler have done it? And if it was not some imposter, the question was even more delicate: What was Doruntine hiding? He paced back and forth in his office; when he came near the window he could see the messenger's back, shrinking steadily as he threaded his way through the bare poplars. And what if neither of these suppositions was correct, he suddenly said to himself. What if something else had happened, something the mind cannot easily comprehend?

He stopped for a moment, his eyes fixed on one particular spot on the floor, then suddenly he made for the door, hurried down the stairs, hailed his deputy on the way down the hallway, and went out into the street.

"Let's go to the church," he said to his deputy when he heard the man's footsteps, then his panting, at his back. "Let's have a look at Constantine's grave."

"A good idea. When all is said and done, the story makes sense only if someone came back from the grave."

"I'm not thinking of anything so insane. I have something else in mind."

His stride lengthened as he said to himself, why am I taking this business so much to heart? After all, there had been no murder, no serious crime, nor indeed any offense of the kind he was expected to investigate in his capacity as regional captain. A few moments ago, as he was drafting his report, this thought had come to him several times: Am I not being too hasty in troubling the Prince's chancellery about a matter of no importance? But some inner voice told him he was not. That same voice told him that something outrageous had occurred, something that went beyond mere murder or any other crime, something that made assassination and similar heinous acts seem mere trifles.

The little church, with its freshly repaired bell tower, was now very near, but Stres suddenly veered off and went straight into the cemetery, not through the iron grille, but through an inconspicuous wooden gate. He had not been in the cemetery for a long time, and he had trouble getting his bearings.

"This way," said his deputy as he strode along, "the graves of the Vranaj sons must be over here."

Stres fell in step beside him. The ground was soft in places. Small icons, half-blackened where candle wax had dripped, exuded quiet sadness. Some of the graves were overgrown with moss. It must be very cool here in summer, Stres thought.

The deputy, who had gone on ahead of him, was walking among the graves, looking this way and that. Stres stooped to right an overturned cross, but it was heavy and he had to leave it. He walked on. He saw his deputy beckon in the distance: he had found them at last.

Stres approached him. The graves, neatly aligned and covered with slabs of black stone, were identical. Their shape was reminiscent of a cross, a sword, or a man standing with his arms stretched out. At the head of each grave was a small niche for an icon and candles. Under it the dead man's name was carved.

"There's his grave," said the deputy, his voice hushed. Stres looked up and saw that the man had gone pale.

"What's the matter?"

His deputy pointed at the grave.

"Take a good look," he said. "The stones have been moved."

"What?" Stres leaned forward to see what his aide was pointing to. For a long moment he examined the spot carefully, then stood up straight. "Yes, it's true. Something's been disturbed here."

"Just as I told you," said the deputy, his satisfaction in seeing that his chief shared his view mixed with a new surge of fear.

"But after all, that doesn't mean much," Stres remarked.

His deputy turned, disconcerted. His eyes seemed to say, sure, a commander must preserve his dignity in all circumstances, but there comes a time to forget about rank, duty, and all that.

"No, it doesn't mean anything," Stres said. "For one thing, the slabs could have tipped over by themselves, as happens eventually in most graves. Moreover, even if someone did move them, it might well have been an unknown traveler who moved the gravestones before perpetrating his hoax in order to make it seem more plausible that the dead man had risen from his grave."

The deputy listened open-mouthed. He was about to say something, perhaps to raise some objection, but Stres went on talking.

"In fact, it is more likely that he did it after leaving Doruntine near the house. It's possible he came here then and moved the gravestones before he went off."

Stres, who now seemed weary, let his gaze wander over the field that stretched before him, as if seeking the direction in which the unknown traveler had ridden off. From where they stood they could see the two-story Vranaj house, part of the village, and the highway, which disappeared into the horizon. It was here on this ground, between the church and that house of sorrow, that the mysterious event of the night of October eleventh had occurred. *Go on ahead. I have something to do at the church. . . .*

"That's how it must have happened," Stres said. "Unless Doruntine is lying."

His deputy kept staring at him. Little by little the color had returned to his cheeks.

"I will find that man," Stress said suddenly. The words came harshly through his teeth, with a menacing ring, and his deputy, who had known Stres for years, felt that the passion his chief brought to the search for the unknown man went well beyond the duties of his office.

CHAPTER II

Stres issued an order that reached all the inns and most relay-stations along the roads and waterways before the day was out. In it he asked that he be informed if anyone had seen a man and woman riding the same horse or two separate mounts, or traveling together by some other means, before midnight on October eleventh. If so, he wanted to be told which roads they had taken, whether they had stayed at an inn, whether they had ordered a meal for themselves or fodder for their horse or horses, and, if possible, what their relationship seemed to be. Finally, he also wanted to know whether anyone had seen a woman traveling alone.

"They can't escape us now," Stres said to his deputy when the chief courier reported that the circular containing the order had been sent to even the most remote outposts. "A man and a woman riding on the same horse. Now that was a sight you wouldn't forget, would you? For that matter, seeing them on two horses ought to have had more or less the same effect."

"That's right," his deputy said.

Stres stood up and began pacing back and forth between his desk and the window.

"We should certainly find some sign of them, unless they sailed in on a cloud."

His deputy looked up.

"But that's exactly what this whole affair seems to amount to: a journey in the clouds!"

"You still believe that?" Stres asked with a smile.

"Everyone believes that," his aide replied.

"The others can believe what they like, but we can't."

A gust of wind suddenly rattled the windows, and a few drops of rain splattered against them.

"The middle of autumn," Stres said thoughtfully. "I have always noticed that the strangest things seem to happen in autumn."

The room grew silent. Stres propped his forehead with his right hand and stood for a moment watching the fine rain fall. But of course he could not stay like that for long. Through the emptiness of his thoughts, the question rose again, persistent, pressing: who could that unknown horseman have been? Within a few minutes dozens of possibilities crossed his mind. Clearly, the man was aware, if not of every detail, at least of the depth of the tragedy that had befallen the Vranaj family. He knew of the death of the brothers, and of Constantine's *bessa*. And he knew the way from that central European region to Albania. But why? Stres almost shouted. Why had he done it? Had he hoped for some reward? Stres opened his mouth wide, feeling that the movement would banish his weariness. The notion that the motive had been some expected reward seemed crude, but not wholly out of the question. Everyone knew that after the death of her sons, the Lady Mother had sent three letters to her daughter, one after the other, imploring her to come to her. Two of the messengers had turned back, claiming that it had been impossible to carry out their mission: the distance was too great, and the road passed through warring lands. In keeping with their agreement with her, they refunded the old woman half the stipulated fee. The third messenger had simply disappeared. Either he was dead or he had reached Doruntine but she had not believed him. More than two years had passed since then, and the possibility that he had brought her back so long after he set out was more than remote. Perhaps the mysterious traveler meant to extort

31

some reward from Doruntine, but had been unable to pass himself off to her as Constantine. No, Stres thought, the reward theory doesn't stand up. But then why had the unknown man gone to Doruntine in the first place? Was it just a commonplace deception, an attempt to kidnap her and sell her into slavery in some god-forsaken land? But that made no sense either, for he had in fact brought her back. The idea that he had set out with the intention of kidnapping her and had changed his mind en route seemed incredible to Stres, who understood the psychology of highwaymen. Unless it was a family feud, some vendetta against her house or her husband's. But that seemed implausible too. Doruntine's family had been so cruelly stricken by fate that human violence could add nothing to its distress. Nevertheless, a careful consultation of the great family's archives—the testaments, acts of succession, ancient trials—might be prudent. Perhaps something could be found that would shed a ray of light on these events. But what if it was only the trick of an adventurer who simply felt like trooping across the plains of Europe with a young woman of twenty-three in the saddle? Stres breathed a deep sigh. With all his soul he wanted to believe it, but he just couldn't. Something held him back, maybe his long years at the trade, in the course of which he had dedicated himself to hunting down crime and solving mysterious cases.

A thousand ideas whirled through his mind, but

he kept coming back to the same question: who was this night rider? Doruntine claimed that she had not seen him clearly at first; she thought he was Constantine, but he was covered with dust, and almost unrecognizable. He had never dismounted, had declined to meet anyone from his brother-in-law's family (though they knew each other, for they had met at the wedding), and had wanted to travel only by night. So he was determined to keep himself hidden. Stres had forgotten to ask Doruntine whether she had ever caught a glimpse of the man's face. He absolutely had to ask her that question. In any event, it could not reasonably be doubted that the traveler had been careful to conceal his identity. It was insane to imagine that it could really have been Constantine, although that was by no means the only issue at stake here. Obviously he wasn't Constantine, but by this time Stres was even beginning to doubt that the girl was Doruntine.

He pushed the table away violently, stood up and left in haste, striding across the field. The rain had stopped. Here and there the weeping trees were shaking off the last shining drops. Stres walked with his head down. He reached the door of the Vranaj house faster than he would have thought, strode through the long corridor where those who had come to attend the two unfortunate women were even more numerous, and entered the room where they both languished. From the door he saw Doruntine's pale face, purple ringing her staring eyes. How could he have doubted it? Of course it was she, with that look, with those same features which that far-off marriage had not changed at all, except perhaps to sprinkle them with some intangible mystery.

"How do you feel?" he asked softly as he sat down beside her, already regretting the doubts he had harbored.

Doruntine's eyes were riveted on him. There was something unbearable in them, and Stres was the first to look away.

"I'm sorry to have to ask you this question," he said, "but it's very important. Please understand me, Doruntine, it's important for you, for your mother, for all of us. I want to ask you whether you ever saw the face of the man who brought you back."

Doruntine still stared at him.

"No," she finally answered, her voice very faint.

Stres sensed a sudden rift in the delicate relations between them. He had a mad desire to seize her by the shoulders and shout, Why don't you tell me the truth! How could you have traveled for days and nights with a man you believed was your brother without ever looking into his face? Didn't you want to see him again? To kiss him?

"How can that be?" he asked.

"When he said that he was Constantine and that he had come to get me I was so confused that a terrible dread seized me."

34

"You thought something bad had happened?"

"Of course. The worst thing. Death."

"First that your mother was dead, then that it was one of your brothers?"

"Yes, each of them in turn, including Constantine."

"Is that why you asked him why he had mud in his hair and smelled of sodden earth?"

"Yes, of course."

Poor woman, thought Stres. He imagined the horror she must have felt if she thought, even for an instant, that she was riding with a dead man. For it seemed she must have spent a good part of the journey haunted by just that fear.

"There were times," she went on, "when I drove the idea from my mind. I told myself that it really was my brother, and that he was alive. But . . . ."

She stopped.

"But . . . ," Stres repeated. "What were you going to say?"

"Something stopped me from kissing him," she said, her voice almost inaudible. "I don't know what."

Stres stared at the curve of her eyelashes, which fell now to the ridge of her cheekbones.

"I wanted so much to take him in my arms, yet I never had the courage, not even once."

"Not even once," Stres repeated.

"I feel such terrible remorse about that, especially now that I know he is no longer of this world."

There was more life in her voice now, her breathing was more rapid.

"If only I could make that journey again," she sighed, "if only I could see him just once more!"

She was absolutely convinced that she had traveled in the company of her dead brother. Stres wondered whether he ought to let her believe that or tell her his own suspicions.

"So, you never saw his face," he said. "Not even when you parted and he said, 'Go on ahead, I have something to do at the church'?"

"No, not even then," she said. "It was very dark and I couldn't see a thing. And during the journey I was always behind him."

"But didn't you ever stop. Didn't you stop to rest anywhere?"

She shook her head.

"I don't remember."

Stres waited until her eyes, still fastened on his own, had recovered their fixed stare.

"But didn't you say that he could have been hiding something from you?" Stres asked. "He didn't want to set foot on the ground, even when he came to get you; he never so much as turned his head during the whole journey; and judging by what you've told me, he wanted to travel only by night. Wasn't he hiding something?"

She nodded.

"I thought about that," she replied, "but since he

was dead, it was only natural for him to hide his face from me."

"Or maybe it wasn't Constantine," he said suddenly.

Doruntine looked at him a long while.

"It comes to the same thing," she said, her voice calm.

"What do you mean, the same thing?"

"If he was not alive, then it's as if it wasn't him."

"That's not what I meant. Did it ever occur to you that this man may not have been your brother, alive or dead, but an imposter, a false Constantine?"

Doruntine gestured no.

"Never," she said.

"Never?" Stres repeated. "Try to remember."

"I might think so now," she said, "but that night I never had any such doubt, not for a moment."

"But now you might?"

As she stared deeply into his eyes once more, he tried to decide just what it was that dominated that look of hers: grief, terror, doubt, some painful longing. All these were present, but there was more; there was still room for something more, some feeling indecipherable, or seemingly indecipherable, perhaps because it was a mixture of all the others.

"Maybe it wasn't him," Stres said again, moving his head closer to hers and looking into her eyes as though into the depths of a well. A wetness of tears rose up. She was crying again.

"I don't know what to do," she said between sobs.

He let her cry in silence for a while, then took her hand, pressed it softly and, after glancing at the mother, who seemed to be sleeping in the other bed, left noiselessly.

The first reports from the innkeepers began to come in two days later. Nowhere had anyone seen a man and woman riding on the same horse or on two horses, nor a woman traveling alone, either on horseback or in a carriage. Although no reports had yet arrived from the most distant inns, Stres was irritated. He had been sure that he would find some trace of them at once. Is it possible, he wondered as he read the reports. Could it be that no human eye had spotted them? Was everyone asleep as they rode through the night? No, impossible, he told himself in an effort to boost his own morale. Tomorrow someone would surely come forward and say that he had seen them. If not tomorrow then the next day. He was sure he would find some seeing eye.

In the meantime, acting on Stres's orders, his deputy was sifting carefully through the family archives, seeking some thread that might lead to the solution to the puzzle. At the end of his first day's work, his eyes swollen from going through a great pile of documents, he reported to his chief that the task was damnable and that he would have preferred to have been sent out on the road, from inn to inn, seeking the trail of the fugitives rather than torturing himself with those archives. The Vranaj were one of the oldest families of Albania, and had kept documents for two hundred and sometimes three hundred years. These were written in a variety of languages and alphabets, from Latin to Albanian, from Cyrillic to Gothic. There were old deeds, wills, legal judgments, notes on the genealogy of the family that went back as far as the year 881, citations, decorations. The documents included correspondence about marriages. There were dozens of letters, and Stres's deputy set aside the ones dealing with Doruntine's marriage, intending to examine them at his leisure. Some of them had been drafted in Gothic characters, apparently in German, and sent to Bohemia. Others, and these seemed to him even more noteworthy, were copies of letters sent by the Lady Mother to her old friend Count Thopia, lord of the neighboring principality, from whom, it seemed, she requested advice about various family matters. The Count's answers were in the archives too. In two or three letters over which Stres's aide cast a rapid eye, the Lady Mother had in fact confessed to the Count her reservations about Doruntine's marriage to a husband from so far away, soliciting his view of the matter. In one of them—it must have been among the most recent—she complained about her terrible loneliness, the words barely legible (one felt that it had been written in a trembling hand, at an advanced age). The brides of her sons had departed one by one, taking their children with them and leaving her alone in the world. They had promised to come back to visit her, but none had done so, and in some sense she felt she could hardly blame them. What young woman would want to return to a house that was more ruin than home and on which, it was said, the seal of death had been fixed?

Stres listened attentively to his deputy, although the latter had the impression that his chief's attention sometimes wandered.

"And here?" Stres finally asked, "what are they saying here?"

The deputy looked at him, puzzled.

"Here," Stres repeated. "Not in the archives, but here among the people, what are they saying about it?"

His deputy raised his arms helplessly.

"Naturally, everyone is talking about it."

Stres let a moment pass before adding, "Yes, of course. That goes without saying. It could hardly be otherwise."

He closed his desk drawer, pulled on his cloak and left, bidding his deputy good night.

His path home took him past gates and fences of the one-story houses that had sprung up since the town, not long ago as small and quiet as the surrounding villages, had become the regional center.

The porches on which people whiled away the summer evenings were deserted now, and only a few chairs or swings had been left outside in the apparent hope of another mild day or two before the rigors of winter set in.

But though the porches were empty, young girls, sometimes in the company of a boy, could be seen whispering at the gates and along the fences. As Stres approached, they interrupted their low masses and watched him pass with curiosity. The events of the night of October eleventh had stirred everyone's imagination, girls and young brides most of all. Stres guessed that each one must now be dreaming that someone—brother or distant friend, man or shadow—would some day cross an entire continent for her.

"So," his wife said to him when he got home, "have you finally found out who she came back with?"

Taking off his cloak, Stres glanced covertly at her, wondering whether there was not perhaps a touch of irony in her words. Tall, blond, she looked back at him with the hint of a smile, and in a fleeting instant it occurred to Stres that though he was by no means insensitive to his wife's charms, he could not imagine her riding behind him, clinging to him in the saddle. Doruntine, on the other hand, seemed to have been born to ride like that, hair streaming in the wind, arms wrapped around her horseman.

"No," he said drily.

"You look tired."

"I am. Where are the children?"

"Upstairs playing. Do you want to eat?"

He nodded yes and lowered himself, exhausted, into a chair covered with a shaggy woolen cloth. In the large fireplace tepid flames licked at two big oak logs but were unable to set them ablaze. Stres sat and watched his wife moving back and forth.

"As if all the other cases were not enough, now you have to search for some vagabond," she said through a clinking of dishes.

She made no direct reference to Doruntine, but somehow her hostility came through.

"Nothing I can do about it," said Stres.

The clinking of dishes got louder.

"Anyway," his wife went on, "why is it so important to find out who that awful girl came home with anyway?" This time the reproach was aimed in part at Stres.

"And what makes her so awful?" he said evenly.

"What, you don't think so? A girl who spends three years wallowing in her own happiness without so much as a thought for her poor mother stricken with the most dreadful grief? You don't think she's an ingrate?"

Stres listened, head down.

"Maybe she didn't know about it."

"Oh, she didn't know? And how did she happen to remember so suddenly three years later?"

Stres shrugged. His wife's hostility to Doruntine was nothing new. She had shown it often enough; once they had even fought about it. It was two days after the wedding, and his wife had said, "How come you're sitting there sulking like that? Are all of you so sorry to see her go?" It was the first time she had ever made such a scene.

"She left her poor mother alone in her distress," she went on, "and then suddenly took it into her head to come back just to rob her of the little bit of life she had left. Poor woman! What a fate!"

"It's true," Stres said, "such a desert—"

"Such a hellish solitude, you mean," she broke in. "To see her daughters-in-law leave one after the other, most of them with small children in their arms, her house suddenly dark as a well. But her daughters-in-law, after all, were only on loan, and though they were wrong to abandon their mother-in-law in her time of trouble, who can cast a stone at them when the first to abandon the poor woman was her only daughter?"

Stres sat looking at the copper candelabrum, astonishingly similar to the ones he had seen that memorable morning in the room where Doruntine and her mother languished. He now realized that everyone, each in his own way, would take some stand in this affair, and that each person's attitude would have everything to do with his station in life, his luck in love or marriage, his looks, the measure of good or ill fortune that had been his lot, the events that had marked the course of his life, and his most secret feelings, those a person sometimes hides even from himself. Yes, that would be the echo awakened in these people by what had happened, and though they would believe they were passing judgment on someone else's tragedy, in reality, they would simply be giving expression to their own.

In the morning a messenger from the prince's chancellery delivered an envelope to Stres. Inside was a note stating that the prince, having been informed of the events of October eleventh, ordered that no effort be spared in bringing the affair to light so as to forestall what Stres himself feared, any uneasiness or misapprehension among the people.

The chancellery asked that Stres notify the prince the moment he felt that the matter had been resolved.

"Hmm," Stres said to himself after reading the laconic note a second time. The moment he felt that the matter had been resolved. Easy enough to say. I'd like to see you in my shoes.

He had slept badly, and in the morning he again encountered the inexplicable hostility of his wife, who had not forgiven him for failing to endorse her judgment of Doruntine with sufficient ardor, though he had been careful not to contradict her. He had noticed that this sort of friction, though it did not lead to explosions, was in fact more pernicious than an open dispute, which was generally followed by reconciliation. Friction of this kind, on the contrary, could fester for days on end in search of good reasons to rise to the surface. And since the pretext was usually irrelevant and unjustified, the resentments and misunderstandings aroused by it were far more bitter than the consequences of any ordinary quarrel.

Stres was still holding the letter from the chancellery when his deputy came in to tell him that the cemetery guard had something to report.

"The cemetery guard?" Stres said in astonishment, eying his aide reproachfully. He was tempted to ask, "You're not still trying to convince me that someone has come back from the grave?"—but just then, through the half-open door, he saw a man who seemed to be the guard in question.

"Bring him in," Stres said coldly.

The guard entered, bowing deferentially.

"Well?" said Stres looking up at the man, who stood rigid as a post.

The guard swallowed.

"I am the guard at the church cemetery, Mister Stres, and I would like to tell you—"

"That the grave has been violated?" Stres interrupted. "I know all about it."

The guard looked at him, taken aback.

"I, I," he stammered, "I want to say—"

"If it's about the gravestone being moved, I know

45

all about it," Stres interrupted again, unable to hide his annoyance. "If you have something else to tell me, I'm listening."

Stres expected the guard to say, No, I have nothing to add, and had already leaned over his desk again when, to his great surprise, he heard the man's voice.

"I have something else to tell you."

Stres raised his head and looked sternly at the man, making it clear that this was neither the time nor the place for jokes.

"So you have something else to tell me?" he said in a skeptical tone. "Well, let's hear it."

The guard, still disconcerted by the coolness of his reception, watched Stres lift his hands from the papers spread out on his desk as if to say, Well, you've taken me away from my work, are you satisfied? Now let's hear your little story.

"We are uneducated people, Mister Stres," the man said timidly. "Maybe I don't know what I'm talking about, please excuse me, but I thought that, well, who knows—"

Suddenly Stres felt sorry for the man and said in a milder tone, "Speak. I'm listening."

What's the matter with me? he wondered. Why do I take out on others the irritation I feel over this business?

"Speak," he said again. "What is it you have to tell me?"

The guard, somewhat reassured, took a deep breath and began.

"Everyone claims that one of the Lady Mother's sons came back from the grave," he said, eyes fixed on Stres. "You know more about all that than I do. Some people have even come over to the cemetery to see whether any stones have been moved, but that's another story. What I wanted to say is about something else—"

"Go on," said Stres.

"One Sunday, not last Sunday or the one before, but the one before that, the Lady Mother came to the cemetery, as is her custom, to light candles at the graves of each of her sons."

"Three Sundays ago?" Stres asked.

"Yes, Mister Stres. She lit one candle for each of the other graves, but two for Constantine's. I was standing very near her at the time, and I heard what she said when she leaned toward the niche in the gravestone."

The guard paused briefly again, his eyes still riveted on the captain. Three Sundays ago; in other words, Stres thought to himself, not knowing quite why he made the calculation, a little more than two weeks ago. "I have heard the lamentations of many a mother," the guard went on, "hers included. But never have I shuddered as I did at the words she spoke that day."

Stres, who had raised his hand to his chin, listened with the greatest attention.

"These were not the usual tears and lamentations," the guard explained. "What she spoke was a curse."

"A curse?"

The guard took another deep breath, making no attempt to conceal his satisfaction at having finally caught the captain's undivided attention.

"Yes, sir, a curse, and a frightful one."

"Go on," Stres said impatiently. "What kind of curse?"

"It is hard to remember the exact words, I was so shaken, but it went something like this: 'Constantine, have you forgotten your promise to bring Doruntine back to me whenever I longed for her?' As you probably know, Mister Stres, I mean almost everybody does, Constantine had given his mother his *bessa* to—"

"I know, I know," said Stres. "Go on."

"Well, then she said: 'Now I am left alone in the world, for you have broken your promise. May the earth never receive you!' Those were her words, more or less."

The guard had been watching Stres's face as he spoke, expecting the captain to be horrified by his terrible tale, but when he had finished, it seemed clear that Stres was thinking of other things. The guard's self-assurance vanished.

"I thought I ought to come and tell you, that it

might be useful to you," he said. "I hope I have not disturbed you."

"No, not at all," Stres hastened to answer. "On the contrary, you did well to come. Thanks very much."

The guard bowed and left, still wondering whether or not he had made a mistake in coming to tell his story.

Stres still seemed lost in thought. A moment later, he felt another presence in the room. He looked up and saw his deputy, but then forgot about him immediately. How could we have been so stupid, he said to himself. Why in the world didn't we talk to the mother? Though he had gone twice to the house, he had questioned only Doruntine. The mother might well have her own version of the incident. It was an unpardonable idiocy not to have spoken to her.

Stres looked up. His deputy stood before him, waiting.

"We have committed an inexcusable blunder," Stres said.

"About the grave? To tell you the truth, I did think of it, but—"

"What are you babbling about?" Stres interrupted. "It has nothing to do with the grave and all these ghost stories. The moment the guard told me of the old woman's curse, I said to myself: how can we account for our failure to talk to her? How could we have been such idiots?"

"That's a point," said the deputy, his tone guilty. "You're right."

Stres stood suddenly.

"Let's go," he said. "We must correct that mistake as soon as possible."

A moment later they were in the street. His deputy tried to match Stres's long strides.

"It's not only the curse," Stres said. "We have to find out what the mother thinks of the affair. She might be able to shed new light on the mystery."

"You're right," said the deputy, whose words, punctuated by his panting, seemed to fly off to float in the wind and fog. "Something else struck me while I was reading those letters," he went on. "Certain things can be gleaned from them—but I won't be able to explain until later. I'm not quite sure of it yet, and since it's so out of the ordinary—"

"Oh?"

"Yes. Please don't ask me to say more about it just yet. I want to finish going through the correspondence. Then I'll give you my conclusions."

"For the time being, the main thing is to talk to the mother," Stres said.

"Yes, of course."

"Especially in view of the curse the cemetery guard told us about. I don't think he would have invented that."

"Certainly not. He's an honest, serious man. I know him well."

"Yes, especially because of that curse," Stres repeated. "For if we accept the fact that she uttered that curse, then there is no longer any reason to believe that when Doruntine said, from outside the house, 'Mother, open the door, I've come back with Constantine' (assuming she really spoke those words), the mother believed what she said. Do you follow me?"

"Yes. Yes I do."

"The trouble is, there's another element here," Stres went on without slowing his pace. "Did the mother rejoice to see that her son had obeyed her and had risen from the grave or was she sorry to have disturbed the dead? Or is it possible that neither of these suppositions is correct, that there was something even darker and more troubling."

"That's what I think," said the deputy.

"That's what I think too," added Stres. "The fact that the old mother suffered so severe a shock suggests that she had just learned of a terrible tragedy."

"Yes, just so," said the aide. "That tallies with the suspicion I mentioned a moment ago—"

"Otherwise there's no explanation for the mother's collapse. Doruntine's is understandable at bottom, for now she learns of the death of her nine brothers. The mother's, on the other hand, is harder to understand. Wait a minute, what's going

51

on here?"

Stres stopped short.

"What's going on?" he repeated. "I think I hear shouts—"

They were not far from the Vranaj house and they peered at the old house.

"I think I do, too," said the aide.

"Oh my God," said Stres, "I hope the old woman's not dead! What a ghastly mistake we've made!"

He set off again, walking faster. His boots splashed in the puddles and the mud, trampling rotting leaves.

"What madness!" he muttered, "what madness!"

"Maybe it's not her," said the deputy. "It could be Doruntine."

"What?" Stres cried, and his aide realized that the very idea of the young woman's death was unthinkable for his chief.

They covered the remaining distance to the Vranaj house without a word. On both sides of the road tall poplars dismally shook off the last of their leaves. Now they could clearly make out the wailing of women.

"She's dead," said Stres. "No doubt about it."

"Yes, the courtyard is thick with people."

"What's happened?" Stres asked the first person they met.

"At the Vranaj's!" the woman said, "both are dead, mother and daughter."

"It can't be!"

She shrugged and walked away.

"I can't believe it," Stres muttered again, slowing his pace. His mouth was dry, and tasted terribly bitter.

The gates of the house yawned wide. Stres and his deputy found themselves in the courtyard surrounded by a small throng of townspeople milling about aimlessly. Stres asked someone else and got the same answer: both of them were dead. From inside came the wailing of the mourners. Both of them, Stres repeated to himself, stunned. So that was the reason for those shrill cries. He had wondered more than once on the way over: why all these cries if it's the old woman? At her age, after all, the end was only natural. But the reality was quite different.

He felt himself being jostled on all sides. He no longer had the slightest desire to pursue the inquiry further, or even to try to think clearly about it. In truth, the idea that it might be Doruntine who was dead had assailed him several times along the road, but he had rejected it each time. He simply could not believe that both no longer lived. At times, even though the idea horrified him, it was Doruntine's death that had seemed to him most likely, for in riding with a dead man, which was what she herself believed she had done, she had already, in some sense, accepted death.

"How did it happen?" he asked no one in particular in that whirlwind of shoulders and voices. "How did they die?"

The answer came from two or three voices at once.

"The daugher died first, then the mother."

"Oh, Doruntine died first?"

"Yes, Captain. And for the aged mother, it's plain that there was nothing left but to close the round of death."

"What a tragedy! What a tragedy!" someone near them said. "All the Vranaj are gone, gone forever!"

Stres caught sight of his deputy, swept along, like himself, in the crowd. Now the mystery is complete, he thought. Mother and daughter have carried their secret to the grave.

He headed for the door of the house to go inside. "The Vranaj are no more!" another voice said. He raised his head to see who had uttered those words, but his eyes, instead of seeking out someone in the small crowd, rose unconsciously to the eaves of the house, as though the voice had come from there. For some moments he did not have the strength to tear his eyes away. Blackened and twisted by storms, jutting out from the walls, the beams of the wide porches expressed better than anything else the dark fate of the line that had lived under that roof.

CHAPTER III

*F*rom the four corners of the principality people flocked to the funeral of the Lady Mother and her daughter. It soon became apparent that this was one of those occasions that, for obscure reasons, people seem to need from time to time so that they may gather together and reaffirm the ties that bind them. Indeed, it had begun on the very day that people first heard of Doruntine's return, but somehow the funeral brought to the surface all that had been whispered or imagined within the walls of every house. Now it coalesced in an endless stream of people, some on foot, others on muleback, still

55

others in carriages, all converging on the region's principal town.

Funeral services had been set for Sunday. The bodies lay in the great reception hall, unused since the death of the Vranaj sons. In the gleam of the candles the family's ancient emblems, the arms and icons on the walls, as well as the masks of the dead, seemed covered with a silver dust.

Beside the majestic bronze coffins (the old mother, in her will, had set aside a large sum for her funeral), four professional mourners, seated on carved chairs, led the lamentations. Twenty hours after the deaths, the wailing of the mourners in the coppery glint of the coffins had become more regular, though more solemn. Now and then the mourners broke their keening with lines of verse. One by one or all four in unison they recalled various episodes in the saga of this unprecedented tragedy.

In a trembling voice, one of the mourners sang of Doruntine's marriage, of her departure for a distant land. A second, her voice more tremulous still, lamented the nine boys who, so soon after the wedding, had fallen in battle against the plague-ridden army. The third took up the theme, and spoke of the grief of the mother left alone. The fourth, recalling the mother's visit to the cemetery to put her curse upon the son who had broken his *bessa,* sang these words:

Constantine, may you be cursed;
Do you remember your *bessa*
Or was it buried with you?

Then the first mourner sang of the resurrection
of the son who had been cursed and of his ride by
night to the land where his married sister lived:

If it's joy that brings you here
I'll dress myself so fair,
If it's grief that brings you here,
A rough-spun dress I'll wear.

while the third responded with the dead man's
words:

Come, my sister, come as you are.

Then the fourth and first mourners, responding
one to the other, sang together of the brother's and
sister's ride, and of the astonishment of the birds
they passed on the way:

Strange things have we seen,
But never the quick and the dead
Riding together thus.

The third mourner told of their arrival at the
house and of Constantine's flight toward the graveyard. Then the fourth concluded the lament, sing-
ing of Doruntine's knocking at the door, of the

words with which she told her mother that her
brother had brought her home, so as to keep his
promise, and of her mother's response from within
the house:

Constantine, poor girl, is dead,
And lying three years in the earth.

After a chorus of lamentations by all the women
present, the mourners rested briefly, then took up
their chants again. The words with which they
punctuated their wailing varied from song to song.
Some verses were repeated, others changed or replaced completely. In these new songs, the mourners passed rapidly over episodes recounted in the
earlier chants, and sometimes lingered over a passage they had previously mentioned only fleetingly
or had omitted entirely. Thus it was that one chant
gave greater prominence to the background of the
incident, to the great Vranaj family's happier days,
the doubts about Doruntine's marriage to a husband from a distant land, and Constantine's promise to bring his sister back whenever their mother
wished. In another all this was recalled but briefly,
and the mourners would linger instead on that dark
ride, recounting the words that passed between
dead brother and living sister. In yet another song
all this was treated more briskly, while new details
were offered, such as her brother's quest for Doruntine as he drifted from dance to dance (for a festival

was under way in Doruntine's village at that time) and what the horseman said of the girls of the village: "Beautiful all, but their beauty left him cold."

The people Stres had sent for the purpose took careful note of the tenor of these laments and reported to him at once. The captain sat near the window through which the cold north wind blew and, seeming numb, examined the reports, taking up his pen and underlining words or even entire lines.

"We might rack our brains night and day to explain what's happened," he said to his deputy. "The mourners carry on their work none the less."

"That's true," his aide replied. "They have no doubt at all that he returned from the dead."

"A legend is being born right before our eyes," Stres said, handing him the sheaf of reports with their underlined passages. "Just look at this. Until two days ago, the songs gave little detail, but since last night, and especially today, they have taken shape as a well-defined legend."

The deputy cast an eye over the pages of underlined verses and words, dotted with brief marginal notes. In places Stres had written question marks and exclamation points.

"Which doesn't mean that we can't get something out of the mourners anyway," he said with the hint of a smile.

"That's right."

In the meantime, people known and unknown flocked to the funeral from all over. There were old friends of the family, relatives by marriage, titled personages and high officials, members of the princely family, and representatives of the Church. August dignitaries of other principalities and counties near and far also came. Count Thopia, the Lady Mother's old friend, unable to make the journey (whether for reasons of ill health or because of a certain chill that had arisen between him and the prince, no one could say), had sent one of his sons to represent him.

The burial took place on Sunday morning as planned. The road was too narrow to accommodate the crowd, and the long cortege made its way with some difficulty to the church. Many were compelled to cross the ditches and cut through the fields. A good number of these people had been guests at Doruntine's wedding not so long ago, and the doleful tolling of the death knell reminded them of that day. The road was the same from the Vranaj house to the church, the same bells tolled, but on this day with a very different sound. There had been almost as many guests at the wedding as now marched in the funeral procession, and then as now, many accompanied the cortege along the edges of the road.

Between Doruntine's marriage and her burial, her nine brothers had died. That was like a nightmare of which no more than a confused memory remains. It had lasted two weeks, the chain of calamity seemingly endless, as though death would be satisfied only when it had closed the door of the house of Vranaj forever. After the first two deaths, which happened on a single day, it seemed as if fate had at last spent its rage against the family, and no one could have imagined what the morrow would bring. No one thought that two more brothers, borne home wounded the evening before, would die just three days later. Their wounds had not seemed dangerous, and the members of the household had thought them far less serious than the afflictions of the two who had died. But when they were found dead on that third day, the family, already in mourning, this new grief compounding the old, was struck by an unendurable pain, a kind of remorse at the neglect with which the two wounded brothers had been treated, at the way they had been abandoned (in fact they had not been abandoned at all, but such was the feeling now that they were dead). They were mad with sorrow—the aged mother, the surviving brothers, the young widowed brides. They remembered the dead men's wounds, which in hindsight seemed to gape. They thought of the care they ought to have lavished on them, care which they now felt they had failed to provide, and they were stricken with guilt. The death of the wounded men was doubly painful, for they felt that they had held two lives in their hands

61

and had let them slip away. A few days later, when death visited their household again with an even heavier tread, carrying off the five remaining brothers, the aged mother and the young widows sank into despair. God himself, people said, doesn't strike twice in the same place, but calamity had struck the house of Vranaj as it had never done to anyone. Only then did people hear that the Albanians had been fighting against an army sick with the plague, and that the dead, the wounded, and most of those who had returned from the war alive would probably suffer the very same fate.

In three months the great house of Vranaj, once so boisterous and full of joy, was transformed into a house of shadows. Only Doruntine, who had left not long before, was unaware of the dreadful slaughter.

The churchbell continued to toll the death-knell, but among the many who had come to this burial it would have been hard to find a single one who had any distinct memory of the funerals of the nine brothers. It had all happened as if in a nightmare, in deep shadow. Coffins were carried out of the Vranaj house nearly every day for more than a week. Many could not recall clearly the order in which the young men had died, and before long would be hard pressed to say which of the brothers fell on the battlefield, which died of illness, and which of the combination of his wounds and the terrible disease.

Doruntine's marriage, on the contrary, was an event each and every one remembered in minute detail, one of those that time has a way of embellishing, not necessarily because they are so unforgettable in and of themselves, but because they somehow come to embody everything in the past that was beautiful, or considered so, but is no more. Moreover, it was the first time a young girl of the country had married so far away. This kind of marriage had stirred controversy since time immemorial. Various opinions were expressed, and there were conflicts, clashes, and tragedies having to do with distance in space and kinship alike, which often coincided. There were those who advocated marriage within clan and *katund,* the village with its hamlets and isolated farms, and some were prepared to uphold this custom at any cost, while others were prepared to fight for the opposite view, that marriages should be concluded at the greatest possible distance. While the first group maintained that home marriages protected the clan against disruption, the second argued the contrary. Indeed, they frightened people by warning of the effects of inbreeding. The two camps fought it out for a long time, and little by little the idea of distant marriages gained the upper hand. But although those who feared inbreeding were easily dissuaded from local marriages, they were equally pained by the prospect of separation. In the beginning, then, the distances were kept small, and marriages two, four, even seven mountains away were countenanced. But then came the striking separation with Doruntine, divided from her family by half a continent.

Now, as the throng following along behind the procession of invited guests headed slowly toward the church, people talked, whispered, recalled the circumstances of Doruntine's marriage, the reluctance of her mother and the brothers who opposed the union, Constantine's insistence that the marriage take place and his *bessa* to his mother that he would always bring Doruntine back to her. As for Doruntine herself, no one knew whether she had freely consented to the marriage. More beautiful than ever, on horseback among her brothers and relatives—who were also mounted—misty with the tears custom requires of every young bride, she already belonged to the horizon more than to them.

All this now came to mind as the procession followed the same path as the throng of guests had taken then. And just as crystal shines the more brightly on a cloth of black velvet, so the memory of Doruntine's marriage against the background of grief now gained in brilliance in the minds of all those present. Henceforth it would be difficult for people to think of the one without the other, especially since everyone felt that Doruntine looked as beautiful in her coffin as she had astride the horse caparisoned for the wedding. Beautiful, but to what end, they murmured. No one had enjoyed her beauty. Now the earth alone would profit from it.

Others, in voices even more muted, spoke of her mysterious return, repeating what people had told them or denying it. It seems, someone said, that Stres is trying to solve the mystery. The prince himself has ordered him to get to the root of it. Believe me, a companion interrupted, there's no mystery about it. She returned to close the circle of death, that's all. Yes, but how did she come back? Ah, that we shall never know. It seems that one of her brothers rose from the grave by night to go and fetch her. That's what I heard, astounding as it may seem. But some people claim that—I know, I know, but don't say it, it's a sin to say such things, especially on the day of her burial. Yes, you're right.

And people cut short their discussions, tacitly agreeing that a few days hence, perhaps even on the morrow, once the dead were buried and tranquility restored, they would speak of this again, and of other things as well, and surely more at their ease.

Which is exactly what happened. Once the burial was over and the whole story seemed at an end, a great clamor arose, the like of which had rarely been heard. It spread in waves through the surrounding countryside and rolled on farther, sweeping to the frontiers of the principality, spilling over its borders and cascading through neighboring principalities and counties. Apparently the many people who had attended the burial had carried bits of it away to sow throughout the land.

Passing from mouth to mouth and ear to ear, the

waves of sound bore, of course, many regrets, of the sort that everyone refrains from expressing directly but is prepared, in such circumstances, to evoke in roundabout ways. And as it grew more distant it began to evaporate, changing shape like a wandering cloud, though its essence remained the same: a dead man had come back from the grave to keep the promise he had made to his mother: to bring his married sister back to her from far away whenever she wished.

Barely a week had gone by since the burial of the two women when Stres was urgently summoned to the Monastery of the Three Crosses. The archbishop of the principality awaited him there, having come expressly on a matter of the greatest importance.

Expressly on a matter of the greatest importance, Stres repeated to himself again and again as he crossed the plain on horseback. What could the archbishop possibly want of him? The prelate rarely left the archiepiscopal seat, and even if there had been some matter that concerned Stres, the archbishop could have spoken to the captain's superiors or summoned him to his headquarters in the principality's capital, thus sparing himself the long journey to the Monastery of the Three Crosses. Perhaps there was some misunderstanding, Stres said to himself, some mixup on the part of officials or messengers. In any event, there was little point in worrying too soon.

A chill wind blew across the plain, which was covered with an autumn frost. On either side of the road all the way to the horizon haystacks seemed to wander bleakly. Stres pulled up the hood of his cloak. What if this was about the Doruntine affair, he said to himself. But he rejected that possibility out of hand. Ridiculous! What had the archbishop to do with that? He had enough thorny problems of his own, especially since the recent paroxysm of tension between the Roman Catholic and Greek Orthodox churches. Some years before, when the spheres of influence of Catholicism and Orthodoxy had become more or less defined, the principality remaining under the sway of the Byzantine church, Stres had thought that this endless quarrel was at last drawing to a close. But not at all. The two churches had once more taken up their struggle for the allegiance of the Albanian princes and counts. Information regularly reported to Stres from the inns and relay stations suggested that in recent times Catholic missionaries had intensified their activities in the principalities. Perhaps that was the reason for the archbishop's visit—but then, Stress himself was not involved in those matters. It was not he who issued safe-conduct passes. No, Stres said to himself, I have nothing to do with that. It must be something else.

He told himself again that he would find out soon enough what it was all about. There was no point in racking his brains now. There was probably a simple explanation: the archbishop may have come for some other reason—a tour of inspection, for example—and decided incidentally to avail himself of Stres's services in resolving this or that problem. The spread of the practice of magic, for instance, had posed a problem for the church, and that did fall within Stres's purview. Yes, he told himself, that must be it, sensing that he had finally found some solid ground. Nevertheless, it was only a small step from the practice of magic to a dead man's rising from his grave. No!—he almost said it aloud—the archbishop must have nothing to do with Doruntine! And spurring his horse, he quickened his pace.

It was very cold. The houses of a hamlet loomed briefly somewhere off to his right, but soon he could see nothing but the plain again, with the haystacks drifting toward the horizon.

The Monastery of the Three Crosses was still far off. Along that stretch of road, Stres kept turning the same ideas over in his mind, but in a different order now. He brought himself up short more than once: nonsense, ridiculous, not possible. But though he resolved repeatedly not to think about it for the rest of his journey, he could not stop wondering why the archbishop had summoned him.

It was the first time Stres had ever been close to the archbishop. Without the chasuble in which

Stres had seen him standing in the nave of the church in the capital, the archbishop seemed thin, slender, his skin so pale, so diaphanous, that you almost felt that you could see what was happening inside that nearly translucent body if you looked hard enough. But Stres lost that impression completely the moment the archbishop started to speak. His voice did not match his physique. On the contrary, it seemed more closely related to the chasuble and miter which he had set aside, but would no doubt have kept by him had they not been replaced by that strangely powerful voice.

The archbishop came straight to the point. He told Stres that he had been informed of an alleged resurrection said to have occurred two weeks before in this part of the country. Stres took a deep breath. So that was it after all! The most improbable of all his guesses had been correct. What had happened, the archbishop went on, was disastrous, more disastrous and far-reaching than it might seem at first sight. He raised his voice. Only frivolous minds, he said, could take things of this kind lightly. Stres felt himself blush and was about to protest that no one could accuse him of having taken the matter lightly, that on the contrary he had informed the prince's chancellery at once, while doing his utmost to throw light on the mystery. But the archbishop, as if reading his mind, broke in:

"I was informed of all this from the outset and issued express instructions that the whole affair be buried. I must admit that I never expected the story to spread so far."

"It is true that it has spread beyond all reason," said Stres, opening his mouth for the first time. Since the archbishop himself admitted that he had not foreseen these developments, Stres thought it superfluous to seek to justify his own attitude.

"I undertook this difficult journey," the archbishop went on, "in order to gauge the scope of the repercussions for myself. Unfortunately, I am now convinced that they are catastrophic."

Stres nodded agreement.

"Nothing less would have induced me to take to the highway in this detestable weather," the prelate continued, his penetrating eyes still riveted on Stres. "Now, do you understand the importance the Holy Church attaches to this incident?"

"Yes, Monsignor," said Stres. "Tell me what I must do."

The archbishop, who apparently had not expected this question so early on, sat motionless for a moment as if choking down an explanation that had suddenly proved unnecessary. Stres felt that the prelate was at the point of exasperation.

"This affair must be buried," he said evenly. "Or rather, one aspect of it, the one that is at variance with the truth, and damaging to the Church. Do you understand me, Captain? We must deny the story of this man's resurrection, reject it, unmask it, prevent its spread at all costs."

"I understand, Monsignor."

"Will it be difficult?"

"Most certainly," said Stres. "I can prevent an imposter or slanderer from speaking, but how, Monsignor, can I stop the spread of this uproar? That is beyond my power."

The archbishop's eyes glittered with a cold flame.

"I cannot prevent the mourners from spinning their yarns," Stres went on, "and as for rumor—"

"Find a way to make the mourners stop their songs themselves," the prelate said sharply. "As for rumor, what you must do is change its course."

"And how can I do that?" Stres asked evenly.

They stared at each other for a long moment.

"Captain," the archbishop finally said, "do you yourself believe that the dead man rose from his grave?"

"No, Monsignor."

Stres had the impression that the archbishop had sighed with relief. How could the man have dreamed that I was naive enough to credit such insanity, he wondered.

"Then you think that someone else must have brought back the young woman in question?"

"Without the slightest doubt, Monsignor."

"Well then, try to prove it," said the archbishop, "and you will find that the mourners will suspend their songs in mid-verse and rumor will change of itself."

"I have sought to do just that, Monsignor," Stres

said. "I have done my utmost."

"With no result?"

"Very nearly. Of course there are people who do not believe in this resurrection, but they are a minority. Most believe it."

"Then you must see to it that this minority becomes the majority."

"I have done all I can, Monsignor."

"You must do even more, Captain. And there is only one way to manage it: you must find the man who brought the young woman back. Find the imposter, the lover, the adventurer, whatever he is. Track him down relentlessly, wherever he may be. Move heaven and earth until you find him. And if you do not find him, then you will have to create him."

"Create him?"

A flash of cold lightning seemed to pass between them.

"In other words," said the archbishop, the first to avert his eyes, "it would be advisable to bear witness to his existence. Many things seem impossible at first that are crowned with success in the end."

The archbishop's voice had lost its ring of confidence.

"I shall do my best, Monsignor," said Stres.

A silence of the most uncomfortable kind settled over the room. The archbishop, head lowered, sat deep in thought. When he next spoke, his voice had changed so completely that Stres looked up sharply, intrigued. His tone, as polite, gentle, and persuasive as the man himself—now matched his physical appearance perfectly.

"Listen, Captain," said the archbishop. "Let us speak frankly."

He took a deep breath.

"Yes, let us speak plainly. I think you are aware of the importance attached to these matters at the Center. Many things are forgiven in Constantinople, but there is no indulgence whatever for any question touching on the basic principles of the Holy Church. I have seen emperors massacred, dragged through the hippodromes, eyes put out, tongues cut out, simply because they dared think they could amend this or that thesis of the Church. Perhaps you remember that two years ago, after the heated controversy about the sex of angels, the capital came close to being the arena of a civil war that might have led to wholesale carnage."

Stres did recall some disturbances, but he had never paid much attention to the sort of collective hysteria which erupted periodically in the Empire's capital.

"Today more than ever," the archbishop went on, "when relations between our Church and the Catholic Church have worsened. . . . Nowadays your life is at stake in matters like these. Do I make myself clear, Captain?"

"Yes," said Stres uncertainly. "But I would like to know what all this has to do with the incident we were discussing."

"Just so," said the archbishop, his voice growing stronger now, recovering its deep resonance, "yes, just so."

Stres kept his eyes fixed upon him.

"Here we have an alleged return from the grave," the prelate continued. "And therefore a resurrection. Do you see what that means, Captain?"

"A return from the grave," Stres repeated. "An idiotic rumor."

"It's not that simple," interrupted the archbishop. "It is a ghastly heresy. An arch-heresy."

"Yes," said Stres, "in one sense it is indeed."

"Not in one sense. Absolutely," the archbishop said, nearly shouting. His voice had recovered its first heavy tones. His head was now so close that Stres had all he could do to keep from leaning back.

"Until now Jesus Christ alone has risen from his tomb! Do you follow me, Captain?"

"I understand, Monsignor," Stres said.

"Well then, He returned from the dead to accomplish a great mission. But this dead man of yours, this Constantine—that is his name, is it not?—by what right does he seek to ape Jesus Christ? What power brought him back from the world beyond, what message does he bring to humanity? Eh?"

Stres, nonplussed, had no idea what to say.

"None whatsoever!" shouted the archbishop. "Absolutely none! That is why the whole thing is nothing but imposture and heresy. A challenge to the Holy Church! And like any such challenge, it must be punished mercilessly."

He was silent for a moment, as if giving Stres time to absorb the flood of words.

"So listen carefully, Captain." His voice had softened again. "If we do not squelch this story now, it will spread like wildfire, and then it will be too late. It will be too late, do you understand?"

Stres returned from the Monastery of the Three Crosses in the afternoon. As his horse trotted slowly along the highway, Stres, with equal languor, mulled over snatches of the long conversation he had just had with the archbishop. Tomorrow I'll have to start all over again, he said to himself. He had, of course, been working on the case without respite, and had even relieved his deputy of his other duties so that he could spend all his time sifting through the Lady Mother's archives. But now that the capital was seriously concerned at the turn of events, he was going to have to go back to square one. He would send a new circular to the inns and relay stations, perhaps promising a reward to anyone who helped find some trace of the imposter. And he would send someone all the way to Bohemia to find out what people there were saying about Doruntine's flight. This latter idea lifted his spirits for a moment. How had he failed to think of it earlier? It was one of the first things he should have done after the events of October eleventh.

Well, he thought a moment later, it's never too late to do things right.

He glanced up to see how the weather looked. The autumn sky was completely overcast. The bushes on either side of the road quivered in the north wind, and their trembling seemed to deepen the desolation of the plain. This world has only one Jesus Christ, thought Stres, repeating to himself the archbishop's words. The sound of his horse's tread reminded him that it was just this long route that Constantine had taken. The archbishop had spoken of the dead man with contempt. Come to think of it, Constantine had never shown much respect for priests while he lived. Stres himself had not known Constantine, but his deputy's research in the family archives had produced some initial clues to his personality. Judging from the old woman's letters, Constantine had been, generally speaking, an oppositionist. Attracted by new ideas, he cultivated them with passion, sometimes carrying them to extremes. He had been like this on the question of marriages. He was against local marriages and, impassioned and extremist in his convictions, had been prepared to countenance unions even at the other end of the world. The Lady Mother's letters suggested that Constantine believed that far-off marriages, hitherto the privilege of kings and princesses, should become common practice for all. The distance between the families of bride and groom was in fact a token of dignity and strength

76

of character, and he persisted in saying that the noble race of Albanians was endowed with all the qualities necessary to bear the trials of separation and the troubles that might arise from them.

Constantine had ideas of his own not only on marriage but on many other subjects as well, ideas that ran counter to common notions and that had caused the old woman more than a little trouble with the authorities. Stres recalled one such instance, which had to do primarily with the Church. Two letters from the local archbishop to the Lady Mother had been found in the family archives in which the prelate drew her attention to the pernicious ideas Constantine was expressing and to the insulting comments about the Church he had occasionally been heard to utter. And there were other, more important matters, his aide had told him, but these would figure in the detailed report he would submit once he had concluded his investigation.

Stres had not been particularly impressed by this aspect of Constantine's personality, possibly because he himself harbored no special respect for religion, an attitude that was in fact not uncommon among the functionaries of the principality. And for good reason: the struggle between Catholicism and Orthodoxy since time immemorial had greatly weakened religion in the Albanian principalities. The region lay just on the border between the two religions, and for various reasons, essentially political and economic, the principalities leaned now toward one, now toward the other. Half of them were now Catholic, but that state of affairs was by no means permanent, and each of the two churches hoped to win spheres of influence from the other. Stres was convinced that the prince himself cared little for religious matters. He had allies among the Catholic princes and enemies among the Orthodox. The principality had once been Catholic, turning Orthodox only half a century before, and the Roman Church had not given up hope of bringing it back to the fold.

Like most functionaries, Stres did his best not to be drawn into religious issues, and he never took the edicts of the Church too seriously. Indeed, he might well have sought some excuse not to respond to the archbishop's summons were it not for the fact that the prince, eager to avoid poisoning relations with Byzantium, had recently issued an important circular urging all officials of the principality to treat the Church with respect. The circular emphasized that this attitude was dictated by the higher interests of the State and that, consequently, any action at variance with the spirit of the directive would be punished.

All this passed through Stres's mind in snatches as his glance embraced the bleak expanse of the plain. The October cold filled the air. Suddenly Stres shivered. Behind a bush several paces off the road he caught sight of the skeleton of a horse standing out in all its whiteness. It was a section of the ribcage and the backbone; the skull was missing. My God, Stres thought to himself a little further on, what if that had been *his* horse?

He drew his cloak tighter around him, trying to drive the image from his mind. He felt sad, but it was not a painful sadness. The shape of his melancholy mood had been softened in the great stretch of plain, in which winter's approach could be read. What possessed you to come out of the earth, what message did you mean to bring us? Stres was astonished at the question, which had risen like a sigh from the depths of his being. He shook his head as if to clear his mind. He who had laughed so derisively at everyone who had believed that story! He smiled bitterly. What nonsense! he said to himself, spurring his horse. What a gloomy afternoon! he thought a moment later. Dusk was falling as he urged his mount into a quicker trot. All the rest of the way to the village he strove to purge his mind of anything connected with the case. He arrived in the dark of night. The lights of the houses shone feebly here and there. The barking of dogs in the distance broke the night silence from time to time. Stres guided his horse not homeward, but toward the town's main street. He had no idea why. Soon he reached the vacant lot that stretched before the house of the Lady Mother. There was no other house to be seen. The dark and dismal mass of the great abandoned building loomed at the far end of a desolate field studded with tall trees that now, in the dark, seemed to droop even more sharply than they really did. Stres approached the doorway, gazed for a moment at the darker rectangles of the windows, then turned his horse in the direction from which he had come. He found himself among the trees. A man standing where he now stood could be seen from the door. The night of October eleventh must have been more or less like this: no moon, but not too dark. It must have been here that Doruntine parted from the unknown horseman. When her mother opened the door, he was probably riding off, but perhaps she had already seen something from the window. Something that caused that fatal shock. Stres turned his horse again. What discovery had the old woman made in the half-darkness? That the man riding off was her dead son? (It was my brother Constantine who brought me back, Doruntine had told her.) Or perhaps, on the contrary, that it was not her son and that her daughter had deceived her. But that would not explain her shock. Or perhaps, just before they separated, Doruntine and the unknown rider had embraced one last time in the dark—Enough! Stres said to himself sharply, and turned his horse back toward the road. At the very last moment, with the furtive movement of a man trying to catch a glimpse of someone spying on him in the darkness, he turned his head toward the closed door once more.

CHAPTER IV

*T*he day after his return from the Monastery of the Three Crosses Stres set to work again to unravel the mystery of Doruntine's return. He drafted a new directive, more detailed than the first, not only ordering the arrest of all suspects but also offering a reward to anyone who helped capture the impostor, whether directly or by providing information leading to his arrest. He also instructed his deputy to make a list of all those who had been out of town between the end of September and the eleventh of October, and to discretely look into the activities of every person on the list. In the meantime, he ordered one of his men to set out at once for the far reaches of Bohemia, in order to investigate on the spot the circumstances of Doruntine's departure.

The man had not yet left when a second directive, even more compelling than the first, came from the prince's chancellery demanding that the entire matter be brought to light as soon as possible. Stres understood at once that the archbishop must have been in touch with the prince and that the latter, aware of his captain's reluctance to obey Church injunctions, had decided that a fresh personal intervention was required. The directive emphasized that the tense political situation of recent times, in particular relations with Byzantium, demanded discretion and understanding on the part of all officials of the prince.

Meanwhile, the archbishop never left the Monastery of the Three Crosses. Why on earth did he hunker there, refusing to budge, Stres wondered. The old fox had obviously decided to stick around and keep an eye on things.

Stres felt more and more nervous. His aide was coming to the end of all that research in the archives. His eyes bleary from the long sessions of reading, he went around looking dreamy. You seem sunk in deep meditation, Stres observed jokingly at a break in his own hectic schedule. Who knows what you're going to pull out of those archives for us? Instead of smiling, the deputy looked strangely at Stres, as if to say: you may think it's a laughing matter, but what I pull out of them will take your breath away.

Sometimes, walking to the window to gaze out at the broad plain, Stres wondered if the truth about Doruntine's tale might not be completely different from what they all assumed, if that macabre ride with an unknown horseman was in fact no more than the product of her own sick mind. After all, no one had seen that horseman, and Doruntine's old mother, who had opened the door for her and who was the only witness, had made no such assertion. Good God, he said to himself, could it be that the whole thing never happened? Perhaps Doruntine had somehow learned of the disaster that had befallen her family and, driven mad by the shock, had set out for home on her own. In a state of such deep distress she might have taken much time indeed—months, even years—to complete a journey she believed had taken a single night. That might well explain the flocks of stars she thought she saw streaming across the sky. Besides, someone who believed that the ten-day-and-night journey from Bohemia (for that was the least it could take) had lasted but a single night might well feel that a hundred nights were one. And of course a person in such a state might fall prey to all sorts of hallucinations.

In vain Stres sought to recall Doruntine's face as it had looked when he saw her for the first time, so that he might detect some sign of mental illness.

But her image eluded him. In the end he resolved to drive the theory of madness from his mind, for he feared it might dampen his zeal for the investigation. It will all be cleared up soon enough, he told himself. As soon as my man comes back from Bohemia.

Thirty-six hours after the man's departure, Stres was informed that some relatives of Doruntine's husband had just arrived. At first it was rumored that her husband himself had come, but it was soon clear that the visitors were his two first cousins.

After dispatching a second messenger to overtake the first and tell him to turn back, Stres hurried to meet the new arrivals, who had taken lodgings at the inn at the crossroads.

The two young men were so alike in bearing and appearance that they might have been taken for twins, though they were not. They were still tired from their long journey and had not yet had time to wash or change their clothes when Stres arrived. He could not help staring at their dust-covered hair, and looked at them in so odd a way that one, with just the hint of a guilty smile, passed his fingers through his hair and spoke a few words in an incomprehensible tongue.

"What language do they speak?" Stres asked his deputy, who had arrived at the inn shortly before him.

"God knows," was the reply. "It sounds to me like German laced with Spanish. I sent someone to the Old Monastery to fetch one of the monks who speaks foreign languages. He shouldn't be long."

"I have a hard time making myself understood with the little Latin I know," said the innkeeper. "And they massacre it too."

"Perhaps they need to wash and rest a bit," Stres said to the innkeeper. "Tell them to go upstairs if they like, until the interpreter gets here."

The innkeeper passed on Stres's message in his fractured Latin. The visitors nodded agreement and, one behind the other, began climbing the wooden stairs, which creaked as if they might collapse. Stres could not help staring at their dust-covered cloaks as he watched them go up.

"Did they say anything?" he asked when the staircase had stopped creaking. "Do they know that Doruntine is dead?"

"They learned of her death and her mother's while on their way here," the deputy answered, "and surely other things as well."

Stres began pacing back and forth in the large hall, which also served as the reception room. The others—his aide, the innkeeper, and a third man—watched him come and go without daring to break the silence.

"This interpreter is taking his time," Stres said three or four times, though he had not been waiting long.

The monk from the Old Monastery arrived half an hour later. Stres immediately sent the innkeeper to fetch the foreigners. One behind the other they descended the wooden stairs, whose creaking seemed more and more sinister to Stres's ear. Their hair, free of most of the journey's dust, looked quite fair.

Stres turned to the monk and spoke.

"Tell them that I am Captain Stres, responsible for keeping order in this district. I believe they have come to find out what happened to Doruntine, have they not?"

The monk translated these words for the strangers, but they looked blankly at one another, seeming not to understand.

"What language are you speaking?" Stres asked the monk.

"I'll try another," he said without answering the question.

He spoke to them again. The two strangers leaned forward with the pained expression of men straining to understand what is being said to them. One of them spoke a few words, and this time it was the monk whose face took on the troubled expression. These exchanges of words and grimaces continued for some time until finally the monk spoke several long sentences to which the strangers now listened with a nod of great satisfaction.

"Finally found it," said the monk. "They speak a German dialect mixed with Slavonic. I think we'll be able to understand one another."

Stres spoke immediately.

"You have come just in time," he said. "I believe you have heard what happened to your cousin's wife. We are all dismayed."

The strangers' faces darkened.

"When you arrived I had already sent someone to your country to find out the circumstances of her leaving there," Stres went on. "I hope that we may be able to learn something from you, as you may learn something from us. I believe that all of us have an equal interest in finding out the truth."

The two strangers nodded in agreement.

"When we left," said one of them, "we knew nothing save that our cousin's wife had gone off suddenly, under rather strange circumstances, with her brother Constantine."

He stopped and waited for the monk, who kept his light-colored eyes fixed upon him, to translate his words.

"While en route," the stranger continued, "when we were still far from your country, we learned that our cousin's wife had indeed arrived at her parents' home, but that her brother Constantine, with whom she said she had left, had departed this life three years ago."

"Yes," said Stres, "that is correct."

"On the way we also learned of the old woman's death, news that grieved us deeply."

The stranger lowered his eyes. A silence followed, during which Stres motioned to the innkeeper and two or three onlookers to go away.

"You wouldn't have a room where we could talk, would you?" Stres asked the owner.

"Yes, of course, Captain. There is a quiet place just over there. Come."

They filed into a small room. Stres invited them to sit on carved wooden chairs.

"We had but one goal when we set out," one of the two strangers continued, "and that was to satisfy ourselves about her flight. In other words, first of all to make sure that she had really gotten to her own family, and second to learn the reason for her flight, to find out whether or not she meant to come back, among other things that go without saying in incidents of this kind."

As the monk translated, the stranger stared at Stres as if trying to guess whether the captain grasped the full meaning of his words.

"For an escapade of this kind, as I'm sure you must realize, arouses. . . ."

"Naturally," said Stres. "I quite understand."

"Now, however," the visitor continued, "another matter has arisen: this question of the dead brother. Our cousin, Doruntine's husband, knows nothing of this, and you may well imagine that this development gives rise to yet another mystery. If Doruntine's brother has been dead for three years, then who was the man who brought her here?"

"Just so," Stres replied. "I have been asking myself that question for several days now, and many others have asked it too."

He opened his mouth to continue, but suddenly lost his train of thought. In his mind, he knew not why, he saw in a flash the white bones of the horse lying on the plain that afternoon, as if they had tumbled there from some troubled dream.

"Did anyone see the horseman?" he asked.

"Where? What horseman?" the two strangers said, together.

"The one believed to have been her brother, the man who brought Doruntine here."

"Oh, I see. Yes, there were women who happened to be close by. They said they saw a horseman near our cousin's house, and that Doruntine hurried to mount behind him. And then there's also the note she left."

"That's true," Stres said. "She told me about a note. Have you read it?"

"We brought it with us," said the second stranger, the one who had spoken less.

"What? You have the note with you?"

Stres could scarcely believe his ears, but the stranger was already rummaging through his leather satchel, from which he finally took out a letter. Stres leaned forward to examine it.

"It's her handwriting, all right," said the deputy, peering over Stres's shoulder. "I recognize it."

Stres, his eyes wide, gaped at the crude letters, which seemed to have been formed by an awkward hand. The text, in a foreign language, was incomprehensible. One word, the last, had been crossed out.

"What does it say?" asked Stres, leaning even closer. Only one word was recognizable, her brother's name, spelled differently than in Albanian: *Cöstanthin*. "What do these other words mean?" Stres asked.

"I am going away with my brother Constantine," the monk translated.

"And the word that's scratched out?"

"It means 'if'."

"So: 'I am going away with my brother Constantine. And if . . .'," Stres repeated. "What was the 'if' for, and why did she cross it out?"

Was she trying to hide something, Stres thought suddenly. Looking for a way to camouflage the truth? Or was this a final attempt to reveal something? But then why did she suddenly change her mind?

"It could be that she found it hard to explain in this language," said the monk, without taking his eyes from the paper. "The other words, too, are full of mistakes."

All were silent.

Stres's thoughts were focused on one point: he finally had a genuine piece of evidence. From all the fog-shrouded anguish there had at last come a piece of paper bearing words written in her own hand. And the horseman had been seen by those women, so he too was real.

"What day did this happen?" he asked. "Do you remember?"

"It was September 29th," one of them answered.

Now the chronology in turn was coming out of that blanket of fog. One very long night, Doruntine had said, with flocks of stars streaming across the sky. But in fact it was a journey of twelve, or more exactly thirteen, days.

Stres felt troubled. The concrete, incontrovertible evidence with which he had just been provided—Doruntine's note, the horseman who had taken her up behind him, the thirteen-day journey—far from giving him any sense that he was finally making some progress and stood on solid ground, left him with no more than a feeling of great emptiness. It seemed that coming closer to the unreal, far from diminishing it, made it even more terrifying. Stres was not sure quite what to say.

"Would you like to go to the cemetery?" he finally asked.

"Yes, of course," chorused the strangers.

They all went together, on foot. From the windows and verandas of the houses, dozens of pairs of eyes followed their path to the church. The cemetery guard had already opened the gate. Stres went through first, chunks of mud sticking to the heels of his boots. The strangers looked absently at the rows of tombstones.

"This is where her brothers lie," said Stres, stopping before a row of black slabs. And here are the graves of the Lady Mother and Doruntine," he continued, pointing to two small mounds of earth into which temporary wooden crosses had been sunk.

The new arrivals stood motionless for a moment, their heads lowered. Their hair now resembled the melted candle-wax on either side of the icons.

"And that grave over there is Constantine's."

Stres's voice seemed far away. The gravestone, canted slightly to the right, had not been straightened. Stres's deputy searched his chief's face, but understood from his expression that he was not to mention that the gravestone had been moved. The cemetery guard, who had accompanied the small group and now stood a little to one side, also held his tongue.

"And there you are," Stres said when they had returned to the road. "A row of graves is all that remains of the whole family."

"Yes, it is very sad indeed," said one of the strangers.

"All of us here were most disturbed by Doruntine's return," Stres went on. "Perhaps even more than you were in your land over her departure."

As they walked they spoke again of the young woman's mysterious journey. Whatever the circumstances, there could be no justification for such a flight.

"Did she seem unhappy in your country?" Stres asked. "I mean, surely she must have missed her family."

"Naturally," one of them answered.

"And at first, I suppose, the fact that she did not know your language must surely have increased her sense of solitude. Was she worried about her family?"

"Very much so, especially in recent times."

In such terrible solitude. . . .

"Especially in recent times?" Stres repeated.

"In recent times, yes. Since none of her relatives had come to visit her, she was in a state of constant anxiety."

"A state of anxiety?" Stres said. "Then surely she must have asked to come herself."

"Oh yes, on several occasions. My cousin had told her, 'If no one from your family comes to see you by spring, I will take you there myself.'"

"Indeed?"

"Yes. And in truth she was not alone in her anxiety, for we had all begun to fear that something might have happened here."

"Apparently she did not want to wait until spring," Stres said.

"It would seem so."

"When he learned of her flight, her husband must surely—"

The two strangers looked at each other.

"Naturally. It was all very strange. Her brother

had come to fetch her, but how was it he had made no appearance at the house, not even for a moment? Admittedly there had been an incident between Constantine and our cousin, but so much time had passed since then—"

"An incident? What sort of incident?" Stres interrupted.

"The day of the wedding," his deputy answered, lowering his voice. "The old woman speaks of it in her letters."

"But notwithstanding this incident," continued the stranger, "her brother's behavior—if indeed it really was her brother—was not justifiable."

"Forgive me," Stres said, "but I wanted to ask you whether her husband thought, even for an instant, that it might not be her brother?"

They looked at each other again.

"Well—how shall I put it? Naturally he suspected it. And needless to say, if it was not her brother, then it was someone else. Anything can happen in this world. But no one would have ever anticipated such a thing. They had been getting along very well. Her circumstances, it must be admitted, were far from easy, being a foreigner as she was, not knowing the language, and especially worrying so much about her family. But they loved each other in spite of everything."

"All the same, to run away like that so suddenly," Stres interrupted.

"Yes, it is strange, we must admit. And it was

just in order to clarify things that, at our cousin's request, we set out on this long journey. But here we have found an even more complicated situation."

"A complicated situation," Stres said. "In one sense that is true enough, but it does not alter the fact that Doruntine actually did come back to her own people."

He spoke these words softly, like a man who finds it difficult to express himself, and in his own heart he wondered, Why on earth do you still defend her?

"That is true," one of the strangers answered. "And in one sense, seen in that light, we find it reassuring. Doruntine indeed came back to her people. But here we have a new mystery: the brother with whom she is said to have made the journey is long since dead. One may therefore wonder who it was that brought her back, for surely someone must have accompanied her here, is that not so? And several women saw the horseman. Why, then, did she lie?"

Stres lowered his head thoughtfully. The puddles in the road were strewn with rotting leaves. He thought it superfluous to tell them that he had already asked himself all these questions. And it seemed equally futile to tell them of his conjecture about an imposter. Now more than ever he doubted its validity.

"I simply don't know what to tell you," he said,

shrugging his shoulders. He felt weary.

"Nor do we know what to say," commented one of them, the one who had so far spoken least. "It is all very sad. We are leaving tomorrow. There is nothing more for us to do here."

Stres did not answer him.

It's true, he thought, his mind numb. There is nothing more for them to do here.

The strangers left the next day. Stres felt as though he had only been awaiting their departure to make a cool-headed attempt, perhaps the last, to clear up the Doruntine affair. It was quite evident that the two cousins had come to find out whether Doruntine had told the truth in her note, since her husband had at first suspected infidelity. And perhaps he had been right. Perhaps the story was far more simple than it appeared, as is often true of certain events which, however simple in themselves, seem to have the power to sow confusion in people's minds, as if to prevent discovery of their very simplicity. Stres sensed that he was finally unraveling the mystery. Up to now he had always assumed that there was an impostor in the case. But the reality was otherwise. No one had deceived Doruntine. On the contrary, it was she who had deceived her husband, her mother, and finally everyone else. She tricked us all, Stres thought with a mixture of exasperation and sorrow.

The suspicion that Doruntine had been lying had

sprung up in his mind from time to time, only to vanish immediately in the mist that surrounded the whole affair. And that was understandable enough, for there were so many unknowns in the case. Stres had only to recall his initial doubts that the horseman and the night ride were real, or his suspicion that Doruntine had actually left her husband's home months, even years, before. Yes, he had only to remember his theory that she had been suffering from mental illness, and all his elegant reasoning seemed merely specious. But the visit of the Bohemian strangers had dispelled all these doubts. Now there was a note, which he had seen with his own eyes, and in it she made mention of her flight with someone. Several women had seen the horseman. And most important of all, a date had been established: September 29th. Now you're stuck, Stres said to himself, not without regret. His satisfaction at the prospect of an early resolution of the mystery was somewhat compromised. Perhaps he had become sentimentally attached to the mystery, and would rather not have seen it brought to light. He even felt himself to have been somehow betrayed.

The whole thing, then, notwithstanding the macabre background, had been no more than a commonplace romance. That was the heart of it. All the rest was secondary. His wife had been right to see it that way from the start. Women sometimes have a special flair for this sort of thing. Yes, that must be it, Stres repeated to himself, as if trying to convince himself as thoroughly as possible. A journey with her lover, though love and sex may well have been blended with grief. But that was just the thing that gave the whole story its special flavor. What wouldn't I give, she had said, to make that journey once more. Yes, of course, Stres said to himself, of course.

He thought of her without resentment, but felt somehow weary. Tentatively at first, then ever more doggedly, his mind began churning in the usual way, trying to reconstruct what might have happened. He thought of the two strangers, now on their way to the heart of Europe and certainly thinking things over just as he was. They must be speaking much more openly between themselves than they did here. They must be mulling over the clues they had turned up themselves or had heard reported by others, the suggestions that this foreign woman, this Doruntine, had had a tendency to deceive her husband.

Little by little Stres filled in the blanks. Sometime after her wedding Doruntine comes to realize that she no longer loves her husband. She sulks, regrets having married him. Her distress is compounded by her ignorance of the language, her solitude, and her yearning for her family. She recalls the long deliberations over this marriage, the hesitation, the arguments pro and con, and all this only deepens her sorrow. To make matters worse, none of her brothers comes to see her. Not even

Constantine, despite his promise. Sometimes she worries, fearing that some misfortune has befallen her family, but she spurns these bleak notions, telling herself that she has the good fortune to have not just one or two brothers but nine, all in the prime of life. She believes it more likely that they have simply forgotten her. They have sent their only sister away, dispatched her beyond the horizon, and now they no longer spare her a thought. Her sadness is paired with mounting hostility toward her husband. She blames him for everything. From the end of the world he had come to fetch her, to ruin her life. Her constant sadness, her lack of joy, becomes tied in her mind with the idea of seeking revenge upon her husband. She resolves to leave him, to go away. But where? She is a young woman of twenty-three, all alone, completely alone, in the middle of a foreign continent. In these circumstances, quite naturally, her only consolation would be some romantic attachment. In an effort to fill the void in her life she initiates one, perhaps not even realizing what she is doing. She gives herself to the first man who courts her. It may have been with any passing traveler (for are not all her hopes bound up with the highway?). Without further thought she decides to go away with him. At first she thinks to run off without a word to anyone, but then, at the last minute, moved by a final twinge of remorse for her husband, or perhaps by mere courtesy (for she was raised in a family that held such rules dear), she decides to leave him a note. Here again she may have hesitated. Should she tell him the truth or not? Probably out of simple human respect, in an effort not to injure his self-esteem, she decides to tell him that she is going away with her brother Constantine. Which is particularly plausible since Constantine had given his *bessa* that he would fetch her on occasions of celebration or grief, and everyone, including her husband, was aware of Constantine's *bessa*.

So, with no other thought in her head, she rides off with her lover. It matters little whether or not they planned to marry. Maybe she meant to return to her family with him sometime later, to explain the situation to her mother and her brothers, to share with them her torment, her solitude (it was so lonely), and perhaps, after hearing her explanation, they might forgive her this adventure and she could live among them with her second husband, never to go away again, never.

But she thinks all this vaguely. Thrilled by her momentary joy, she has no reason to worry too much about what lies ahead. She has time, and later she will see. Meanwhile she roams from inn to inn with her lover (they must have sold her jewelry), drunk with happiness.

But this happiness does not last long. In one of these inns (the things one learns in those inns with their great fireplaces during the long autumn nights!) she hears of the tragedy that has befallen her family. Perhaps she learns the full truth, perhaps only a part, or perhaps she simply imagines what must have happened, for she has heard talk of the foreign army sick with the plague that has ravaged half of Albania. She is near to madness. Remorse, horror, and anguish drive her to the brink of insanity. She begs her lover to take her home right away, and he agrees. So it is she, Doruntine, who leads the unknown horseman, with difficulty finding her way from country to country, from one principality to the next.

The closer they get to the Albanian border, the more she thinks about what she will say when she is asked, "Who brought you back?" Until now she has given the matter little thought. If only she can get home, she will think of something then. But now the family hearth is no longer far off. She will have to account for her arrival. If she says that she was accompanied by an unknown traveler, she has little chance of being believed. To say openly that she came with her lover is also impossible. Earlier she had thought of these things incoherently, bringing little logic to bear, for the issue seemed of scant importance under the burden of her grief. But now it becomes ever more pressing. As her mind goes in every direction looking for a solution, she suddenly recalls Constantine's *bessa* and makes her decision: she will say that Constantine kept his word and brought her home. Which means that she knows that he will not be there, that he is absent, that he is dead. She is not yet aware of the scope of the disaster that has struck her family, but she has learned of his death. Apparently she has asked after him in particular. Why? It is only natural for him to occupy a larger place in her mind than the others, since it was he who had promised to come and fetch her. Through the long days of sorrow in her husband's home she had been waiting for him to appear on the dusty road.

And now the house is near. She is so agitated that she has no time to invent a new lie even if she wanted to. She will say that the dead man brought her back. And so she finally knocks at the door. She tells her lover to stay off to one side, to be careful not to be seen; perhaps she arranges to meet him somewhere several days hence. From within the house her mother asks the expected question: with whom have you come? And she answers: with Constantine. Her mother tells her that he is dead, but Doruntine already knows it. Her lover insists on one last kiss before the door opens, and takes her in his arms in the half-darkness. That is the kiss the old woman glimpses through the window. She is horrified. Does she believe that her son has risen from the grave to bring her daughter back to her? It is a better bet that she assumes that it is not her son, but someone unknown to her. However that may be, whether she thought that Doruntine was kissing a dead man or a living one, she felt equal horror. But there's a good chance that the mother thought she saw her kissing a stranger. Her daughter's lie seems all the more macabre: though in mourning, she takes her pleasure with unknown travelers like a common slut.

No one will ever know what happened between mother and daughter, what explanations, curses, or tears were exchanged once the door swung open.

Events then move rapidly. Doruntine learns the full dimensions of the tragedy, and needless to say loses all contact with her lover. Then the dénouement. Stres's mistake was to have asked, in his very first circular to the inns and relay stations, for information about two riders (a man and woman riding the same horse or two horses) coming into the principality. He should have asked that equal effort be concentrated on a search for any solitary traveler heading for the border. But he had corrected the lapse in his second circular, and he now hoped that the unknown man might still be apprehended, for he must have remained in hiding for some time waiting to see how things would turn out. Even if it proved impossible to capture him here, there was every chance that some trace of his passage would be found, and the neighboring principalities and dukedoms, strongly subject to Byzantium's influence, could be alerted to place him under arrest the moment he set foot in their territory.

Before going home for lunch, Stres again asked his aide whether he had heard anything from the inns. He shook his head no. Stres threw his cloak

103

over his shoulders and was about to leave when his deputy added:

"I have completed my search through the archives. Tomorrow, if you have time, I will be able to present my report."

"Oh? And how do things look?"

His deputy stared at him.

"I have an idea of my own," he replied evenly, "quite different from all current theories."

"Oh?" Stres said again, smiling without looking at the man. "Good-bye, then. Tomorrow I'll hear your report."

As he walked home his mind was nearly blank. He thought several times of the two strangers now riding back to Bohemia, going over the affair in their own minds again and again, no doubt thinking what he, in his own way, had imagined before them.

"You know," he said to his wife the moment he came in, "I think you were right. There's a very strong chance that this whole Doruntine business was no more than an ordinary romantic adventure after all."

"Oh really?" Beneath her flashing eyes, her cheeks glowed with satisfaction.

"Since the visit of the husband's two cousins it's all becoming clear," he added, slipping off his cloak.

As he sat down by the fire, he had the feeling that something in the house had come to life again, an animation sensed more than seen or heard. His wife's customary movements as she prepared lunch were more lively, the rattling of the dishes more brisk, and even the aroma of the food seemed more pleasant. As she set the table he noticed in her eyes a glimmer of gratitude that quickly dispelled the sustained chill that had marked their days recently. During lunch the look in her eyes grew still softer and more meaningful, and after the meal, when he told the children to go take their naps, Stres, stirred by a desire he had felt but rarely in these last days, went to their bedroom and waited for her. She came in a moment later, the same gleam in her eyes, her hair, just brushed, hanging loose upon her shoulders. Stres thought suddenly that in days to come, the dead woman would come back often, either to bring a chill, or, as now, to kindle their flesh.

Later, sated by love, they lay silent for a long moment, glancing now at the carved-wood ceiling, now at the window whose half-open shutters revealed a slice of low late-autumn sky.

"Look," she said, "a stork. I thought they'd gone long ago."

"A few sometimes stay behind. Laggards."

He could not have said why, but he felt that the conversation about Doruntine, suspended since lunch, now threatened to arise again. With a caressing touch that smoothed a lock of her hair on her temple, he turned his wife's eyes from the sky, convinced that he had managed, in this way, to escape any further talk of the dead woman.

The next day Stres summoned his deputy so that he might report on the conclusions he had drawn from examining the Vranaj archives. The man still looked haggard, and Stres thought him even paler than usual.

"As I have said before, and as I repeated to you yesterday," he began, "my research in these archives has led me to a conclusion about this disturbing incident quite different from those commonly held."

I never would have imagined that prolonged contact with archives could give anyone that papier-mâché expression, Stres said to himself.

"And," the deputy went on, "the explanation I have come to is also very different from what you yourself think."

Stres raised his eyebrows in mock astonishment.

"I'm listening," he said as his aide seemed to hesitate.

"This is not a figment of my imagination," the deputy went on. "It is a truth that became clear to me once I had scrupulously examined the Vranaj archives, especially the correspondence between the old woman and Count Thopia."

He opened the folder he was holding and took out a packet of large sheets of paper yellowed by time.

"And just what do these letters amount to?" Stres asked impatiently.

His deputy took a deep breath.

"From time to time the old woman told her friend her troubles, or asked his advice about family affairs. She had the habit of making copies of her own letters."

"I see," said Stres. "But please, try to keep it short."

"Yes," replied his deputy, "I'll try."

He took another breath, scratched his forehead.

"In certain letters, one in particular, written long ago, the old woman alludes to an unnatural feeling on the part of her son Constantine for his sister, Doruntine."

"Really?" said Stres. "What sort of unnatural feeling? Can you be more specific?"

"This letter gives no details, but bearing in mind other things mentioned in later letters, particularly Count Thopia's reply, it is clear that it was an incestuous feeling."

"Well, well."

Thick drops of sweat stood out on the deputy's forehead. He continued, pretending not to notice his chief's ironic tone.

"In fact, the count immediately understood what she meant, and in his reply," said the aide, slipping a sheet of paper across the table to Stres, "he tells her not to worry, for these were temporary things, common at their ages. He even mentions two or three similar examples in families of his acquaintance, emphasizing that it happens particularly in families in which there is but one daughter, as was the case with Doruntine. However, it takes attention and care to bring this somewhat perverse feeling back to normal. In any event, we'll talk about this at length when we see each other again."

The deputy looked up to see what impression the reading had had on his chief, but Stres was staring at the tabletop, tapping his fingers nervously.

"Their subsequent letters make no further mention of the matter," the aide went on. "One has the impression that, as the count predicted, the brother's unhealthy feeling for his sister had become a thing of the past. But in another letter, written several years later, when Doruntine was of marriageable age, the old woman tells the count that Constantine is unable to conceal his jealousy of any prospective fiancé. On his account, she says, we have had to reject several excellent matches."

"And what about Doruntine?" Stres interrupted.

"Not a word about her attitude."

"And then what?"

"Later, when the old woman told the count of the far-away marriage that had just been arranged, she wrote that she herself, Doruntine, and most of her sons had long hesitated, concerned that the distance was too great, but that this time it was Constantine who argued vigorously for the prospective marriage. In his letter of congratulation, the count tells the old woman, in particular, that Constantine's attitude toward the marriage is not at all surprising, that on the contrary, in view of what she had told him it was understandable that Constantine, angered by the possibility of any local marriage which would have forced him to see his sister united with a man he knew, could more easily resign himself to her marriage to an unknown suitor, preferably a foreigner as far out of his sight as possible. It is a very good thing, the count wrote, that this marriage has been agreed upon, if only for that reason."

The deputy leafed through his folder for a few moments. Stres's eyes were fixed on the floor.

"Finally," the aide continued, "we have here the letter in which the old woman described the wedding to her correspondent, and, among other things, the incident that took place there."

"Ah yes, the incident," said Stres, as if torn from his somnolence.

"Though this incident passed largely unnoticed, or in any event was considered natural enough in the circumstances, it was only because people were unaware of those other elements I have just told you about. The Lady Mother, on the other hand, who was well acquainted with these elements, offers the proper explanation of the event. Having written to the count that after the church ceremony Constantine paced back and forth like a madman, that when they had accompanied the groom's kinsmen as far as the highway, he accosted his sister's husband, saying to him: 'She is still mine, do you understand, mine!' the old woman tells her friend that this, thank God, was the last disgrace she would have to bear in the course of this long story."

Stres's subordinate, apparently fatigued by his long explanation, paused and swallowed.

"That's what these letters come to," he said. "In the last two or three, written after her bereavement, the old woman complains of her loneliness and bitterly regrets having married her daughter to a man so far away. There's nothing else. That's it."

The man fell silent. For a moment the only sound came from Stres's fingers tapping on the tabletop.

"And what does all this have to do with our case?"

His deputy looked up.

"There is an obvious, even direct, connection."

Stres looked at him with a questioning air.

"I think you will agree that there is no denying Constantine's incestuous feelings."

"It's not surprising," Stres said. "These things happen."

"You will also admit, I imagine, that his stubborn desire to have his sister marry so far away is evidence of his struggle to overcome that perverse impulse. In other words, he wanted his sister to have a husband as far from his sight as possible, so as to remove any possibility of incest."

"That seems clear enough," said Stres. "Go on."

"The incident at the wedding marks the last torment he was to suffer in his life."

"In his life?" Stres asked.

"Yes," said the deputy, raising his voice for no apparent reason. "I am convinced that Constantine's unslaked incestuous desire was so strong that death itself could not still it."

"Hm," Stres said.

"Incest unrealized survived death," his aide went on. "Constantine believed that his sister's distant marriage would enable him to escape his yearning, but, as we shall see, neither distance nor even death itself could deliver him from it."

"Go on," Stres said drily.

His aide hesitated for a moment. His eyes, burning with an inner flame, stared at his chief, as if to make sure that he had leave to continue.

"Go on," said Stres a second time.

But his deputy was still staring, still hesitating.

"Are you trying to suggest that his unsated incestuous desire for his sister lifted the dead man from his grave?" asked Stres, his voice icy.

"Precisely!" his aide cried out. "That macabre escapade was their honeymoon."

"Enough!" Stres bellowed. "You're talking nonsense!"

"I suspected, of course, that you would not share my view, but that is no reason to insult me, sir."

"You're out of your mind," Stres said. "Completely out of your mind."

"No, sir, I am not out of my mind. You are my superior. You have the right to punish me, to dismiss me, even to arrest me, but not to insult me. I, I—"

"You, you, you what?"

"I have my own view of this matter, and I believe it to be no more than a case of incest, for Constantine's actions can be explained in no other way. As for the theory, which I have lately heard expressed, that he insisted that his sister marry into a distant family because he had some inkling of the calamity that was soon to befall the family and did not wish to see her so cruelly hurt, I consider it absurd. It is true that Constantine harbored dark forebodings, but it was the threat of incest that tormented him, and if he sent his sister away, it was to remove her from this danger rather than to ensure that she would escape a calamity of some other kind . . . ."

The deputy spoke rapidly, not even pausing for breath, lest he be forbidden to continue.

"But as I said, neither distance nor death itself allowed him to escape incest. Thus it was that one stifling night he rose from his grave to do what he had dreamed of doing all his life—let me speak, please, do not interrupt—he rose from the earth on that wet and sultry October night and, mounting his gravestone become a horse, set out to live his life's dream. And thus did that sinister honeymoon

112

journey come about, the girl riding from inn to inn, just as you said, not with a living lover but with a dead one. And it was just that heinous fact that her aged mother discovered before she opened the door. Yes, she saw Doruntine kiss someone in the shadows, not the lover or impostor you believed, but her dead brother. What the old woman had feared all her life had finally happened. That was the disaster she discovered, and that was what brought her to her grave—"

"Madman," said Stres, more softly this time, as though murmuring the word to himself. "I forbid you to continue," he said evenly.

His aide opened his mouth, but Stres leapt to his feet and, leaning close to the man's face, shouted:

"I forbid you to speak, do you hear? Stop or I'll arrest you, here and now. Do you understand?"

"I have spoken my mind," the man replied, breathing with difficulty. "Now I shall obey."

"It's you who are sick," Stres said. "You're the one who's sick, poor man."

He looked a long moment at his deputy's face, pale with insomnia, and suddenly felt keenly sorry for him.

"I was wrong to assign you to all that research in the family archives. So many long hours of reading, for someone unused to books—"

The man's feverish eyes remained fixed on his chief.

"You may go now," said Stres, his tone indulgent. "Get some rest. You need rest, do you hear? I am prepared to forget all this nonsense, provided you forget it too, do you follow me? You may go."

His aide rose and left. Stres, smiling stiffly, watched the man's unsteady gait.

I must find that adventurer right away, he said to himself. The archbishop was right, the whole business should have been nipped in the bud to avoid the dangerous consequences it will surely lead to.

He began to pace the room. He would tighten precautions at every crossing point, assign all his men to the task, suspend all other activity to mobilize them for this one case. He would set everything in motion, he would spare no effort until the mystery was cleared up. I must find the truth, he told himself, as soon as possible. Or else we'll all go mad.

Despite the efforts of Stres's men, acting in concert with Church officiants who lectured the faithful day after day, those who believed that Doruntine had returned with her lover were many fewer than those inclined to think that the dead man had brought her back.

Stres himself examined the list of people who had been out of the district between the end of September and the eleventh of October. The idea that Doruntine might have been brought back by one of Constantine's friends so that his promise might be fulfilled came to him from time to time, but each time it struck him as hardly credible. Even after the complete list of absentees had been submitted to him and he found, as he had hoped, that the names of four of the dead man's closest friends were on it, he could not bring himself to accept the conjecture. After all, hadn't he himself been away on duty during just that time? And in any event, Constantine's friends had little trouble proving that all four had been at the games held annually in Albania's northernmost principality. Two of them had even taken part, and had won prizes.

In the meantime, it would soon be forty days since the death of mother and daughter. The day would be celebrated according to custom, and the mourners would certainly sing their distressing ballads, without changing a damned word. Stres was well acquainted with the obtuse stubbornness of those little old women. On the seventh day after the deaths, also celebrated according to custom, they had changed nothing despite the warning he had sent them, and they had done the same on the four Sundays that followed. The old crows will caw for another few days, the priest had said, but in the end they'll be quiet. But Stres found that hard to believe.

One day he saw them making their way, single file, to the abandoned house to take up their mourning, as was the custom. Tall, slim, wrapped in his dark cloak, its collar emblazoned with the insignia of an officer of the prince—the white deer-antler—he had stopped at the side of the road as, dressed all in black, their faces already moist with the tears to come, they passed before him, indifferent. Stres had the feeling that they had recognized him, for he thought he could detect in their eyes a glint of irony directed at him, the destroyer of legends. He nearly burst out laughing at the thought that he was engaged in a duel with these mourners, but to his astonishment the idea suddenly turned into a shiver.

In the meantime, the archbishop, to everyone's surprise, had remained at the Monastery of the Three Crosses, though Stres was no longer annoyed about it. Absorbed in his pursuit of the wandering adventurer, he paid little attention to anything else. He had received no clear information from the innkeepers. There had been three or four arrests on the basis of their reports, but all the suspects had been released for lack of evidence. Information was awaited from neighboring principalities and dukedoms, especially in the northern districts through which the road to Bohemia passed. At times Stres entertained new doubts and built new theories, only to set them aside at once.

Towards the middle of November the first snow fell. Unlike the snow that falls in October, it did not melt, but blanketed the countryside in white. One afternoon as he was on his way home, Stres, almost unconsciously, turned his horse into the street leading to the church. He dismounted at the cemetery gate and went in, trampling the immaculate snow. The graveyard was deserted, the crosses against the blanket of snow looked even blacker. A few birds, equally dark, circled near the far side of the cemetery. Stres walked until he thought he had found the group of Vranaj graves. He leaned forward, deciphered the inscription on one of the stones, and saw that he had made no mistake. There were no footprints anywhere around. The icons seemed frozen. What am I doing here, he asked himself with a sigh. He felt the peace of the graveyard sweep over him, and the feeling brought with it a strange mental clarity. Dazzled by the glare of the snow, he found himself unable to look away, as if he feared that the clarity might desert him. All at once Doruntine's story seemed as simple as could be, perfectly clear. Here was a stretch of snow-covered earth in which was buried a group of people who had loved one another intensely and had promised never to part. The long separation, the great distance, the terrible yearning, the unbearable solitude (it was so lonely. . . .) had tried them sorely. They had strained to reach one another, to come together in life and in death in a state partaking of death and life alike, dominated now by the one, now by the other. They had tried to flout the laws that bind the living together and prevent them from passing back from death to life; they had thereby tried to violate the laws of death, to attain the inaccessible, to gather together once more. For a moment, they thought they had managed it, as in a dream when you encounter a dead man you have loved but realize that it is only an illusion (I could not kiss him, something held me back). Then, in the darkness and chaos, they parted anew, the living making her way to the house, the dead returning to his grave (you go ahead, I have something to do at the church), and though nothing of the kind had really happened, though Stres still could not bring himself to believe that the dead man had risen from his grave, in some sense that was exactly what had happened. The horseman-brother had appeared at a bend in the road and said to his sister, "Come with me." It mattered little, in truth, whether it was all in her mind or in the minds of others. In the end, it was a story that could happen to anyone, in any land, in any time. For where, indeed, is the person who has never dreamed of someone who returns from afar, from the lands beyond, to pause a moment that both may sit astride the same horse together? Where is the person in this world who does not harbor some yearning for one departed and has never said, If only he could come back one time, just once, that I might kiss him (but something stops me from kissing him)? Even though it can never happen, and will never happen forever and ever, for surely this is one of the great sorrows of this dreary world, a sorrow that will envelop it like mist until its very end.

That's what it was all about, Stres said to himself
again. All the rest—the suppositions, the investigation, all the reasoning—was just a pack of mean
little lies signifying nothing. He would have liked
to linger a while longer on that high ground where
his thought flowed so freely, but he felt a world of
banality drawing him relentlessly downward, ever
faster, making him plunge at once from his flight.
He made haste to leave before his fall was complete.
Haggard, he stumbled like a sleepwalker to his
horse, vaulted into the saddle, and rode off in a
frozen gallop.

CHAPTER V

*I*t was a wet afternoon, drenched in a fine and steady rain, one of those afternoons when one feels that nothing could possibly happen. Stres, dressed and dozing in an armchair (what else could he do on such a day), felt his wife's hand touch his shoulder gently.

"Stres, there are people here to see you."

He woke with a start.

"What is it? Was I sleeping?"

"They're asking for you," his wife said. "It's your deputy, and another man with him."

"Oh? Tell them I'll be right down."

His aide and someone Stres didn't know, their hair dripping, stood waiting on the porch.

"Captain," said his deputy the moment he saw his chief, "the man who brought Doruntine back has been captured."

Stres stood for a moment, stunned.

"How can that be?" he asked.

His deputy was astonished at the surprise evident in the face of his chief, who showed no sign of satisfaction, as if he hadn't spent weeks trying to find the man.

"Yes, they've caught him at last," he said, still not sure whether his chief had fully grasped what he was talking about.

Stres was still looking at them questioningly. In fact he had understood perfectly. What he wasn't sure of was whether or not the news pleased him.

"But how?" he asked. "How could it happen so suddenly?"

"So suddenly?" his deputy said.

"What I mean is, it seemed so unlikely . . . ."

What in the world am I talking about? he said to himself. Then he realized what was troubling him. It seemed that his desire to find the supposed lover had coexisted with another, hidden wish: that the man would never be found. It was then that he turned his attention to the stranger, and, without quite knowing why, addressed him directly.

"But how did they catch him? And where?"

"They're bringing him in now," answered his

deputy. "He'll be here before nightfall. This man is the messenger who brought the news, as well as a report."

The stranger reached into the lining of his leather tunic and took out an envelope.

"He was captured in the next county, in a place called the Inn of the Two Roberts," the deputy said.

"The Inn of the Two Roberts?"

"Here is the re . . . re . . . report," said the stranger, who stuttered.

Stres took it from him brusquely. Little by little the vague feeling of sadness and regret at the resolution of the mystery gave way to a first surge of cold satisfaction. He unsealed the envelope, took out the report, turned it toward the light, and began to read the lines written in a handwriting that looked like a heap of pins thrown down in anger:

We hereby dispatch to you this report on the capture of the adventurer suspected of having deceived and brought back Doruntine Vranaj. The information in this report has been taken from that which has been handed over to our authorities, along with the adventurer in question, by the authorities of the neighboring county, who captured him in their territory, in accordance with the request of our authorities.

The vagabond was arrested on the fourteenth of November in the highway establishment known as the Inn of the Two Roberts. He had been brought there unconscious the night before by two peasants who found him lying in the road burning with fever. His appearance and, in particular, his delirious raving immediately aroused the suspicions of the innkeeper and the customers. The snatches of sentences he spoke amounted more or less to this: "There is no need to hurry so. What will we say to your mother? Hold on tight, I can't go any faster, it's dark, you know, I can't see anything. That's what you'll say if anyone asks you who brought you back. Don't be afraid, none of your brothers is still alive."

The innkeeper alerted the local authorities, who, after hearing his testimony and that of the customers, decided to arrest the vagabond and, in accordance with our request, to hand him over to us at once. In keeping with the instructions that I have received from the capital, I will send him on to you immediately, but I thought it useful also to send you this information by a swift messenger as well, so that you might be fully informed about the matter in case you wish to interrogate the prisoner at once.

I send you my greetings.

Captain Stanish, of the border region.

Stres looked up from the sheet he was holding and glanced quickly at his deputy, then at the messenger. So it was just as he had imagined: she had run off with a lover. Soon he would learn the details from the mouth of the arrested man himself.

"When are they due to arrive?" he asked the messenger.

"In two hours, three at most."

It was only then that Stres noticed that the messenger's boots were caked with mud to the knees. He took a deep breath. The ideas that had come to him in the graveyard snow three days before seemed very far away.

"Wait for me," he said, "while I get my cloak."

He went back inside and, donning his long cloak, told his wife:

"The man who brought Doruntine back has been captured."

"Really?" she said. She could not see his face, for a flap of his cloak, like a great black bird, had fallen between them, and kept their eyes from meeting.

She went as far as the threshold and watched as the three men walked off in the rain, Stres leading the way.

They had been waiting more than two hours for the carriage that was to bring the prisoner. The floorboards creaked plaintively under Stres's boots as he paced back and forth, as was his custom, between his work table and the window. His deputy dared not break the silence, and the messenger slumped snoring in a wooden chair, a musty odor rising from his clothes.

Stres could not help stopping at the window from time to time. As he gazed out at the plain and waited for the carriage to appear, he felt his mind going slowly numb. The same steady and monotonous rain had been falling since morning, and anyone's arrival, from whatever quarter, seemed quite inconceivable under its dreary regularity.

He touched the thick paper of the report with his fingers as if to convince himself that the man he was waiting for was really coming. We can't go any faster, it's dark, you see. He repeated to himself the delirious prisoner's words. Don't be afraid, none of your brothers is still alive. . . .

He's the one, Stres said to himself. Now he was sure of it. Just as he had imagined. He recalled the moment in the cemetery, that day in the snow when he told himself that it was all lies. Well, it wasn't all lies, he now thought, his eyes fixed on the icy expanse. The plain stretched to infinity in the grey rain, and the snow itself had melted or withdrawn into the distance without a trace, as if to help him forget the ideas he had had that day.

The dusk was getting thicker. On either side of the road an occasional idler could be seen, no doubt awaiting the arrival of the carriage. News of the arrest had apparently spread.

The messenger, dozing in his corner, made a sound like a groan. If what he had said was true, Stres thought, they should be here by now. The deputy seemed lost in thought. Stres had heard no further mention of that incest theory of his. He must be embarrassed now.

The messenger let out another groan and half opened his eyes. A madman's eyes, one would have said.

"What's going on?" he asked. "Are they here yet?"

No one answered. Stres went to the window for perhaps the hundredth time. The plain was now so gloomy that it was hard to make out anything. But soon the arrival of the carriage was heralded, first by a far-off rumbling, and then by the clatter of its wheels.

"Good God! They're finally here," said Stres's deputy, shaking the messenger by the shoulder.

Stres ran down the stairs, followed by his aide and the messenger. The carriage was rolling up as they got to the threshold. A few people were following along in the dark. Others could be heard running from farther off. At last the carriage stopped and a man dressed in the uniform of an officer of the prince got off.

"Where is Captain Stres?" he asked.

"I am he," said Stres.

"I believe you have been informed that—"

"Yes," Stres interrupted. "I know all about it."

The man in uniform seemed about to add something, but then turned and headed for the carriage, leaned in through the window, and said a few words to the people inside.

"Light a lantern," someone called out.

The footman opened the carriage door, revealing a pair of booted legs, then a second pair of legs thoroughly spattered with mud. When the bodies that went with the legs appeared, it could be seen that the man covered with dried mud was shackled.

"It's him! It's him!" whispered the people who had gathered around.

The flickering gleam of the lantern revealed no more than half the face of the man in irons, a face bizarrely streaked with mud. The men who had brought him handed him over to two of Stres's men, who took hold of him, as the first ones had, by the armpits. The shackled man offered no resistance.

"To the dungeon," Stres said shortly. "What about you, what do you mean to do now?" he added, addressing the man in uniform, who seemed to be the commander of the small detachment.

"We're going back at once," he replied.

"Are you going with them?" Stres asked the messenger.

"Yes, sir."

Stres stood there until the carriage shook into motion, then turned toward the building. At the very last moment he paused on the threshold. He sensed the presence of people in the half-darkness. In the distance he heard the footsteps of a man running toward them.

"What are you all waiting for, good people?" Stres asked quietly. "Why don't you go home and go to bed? We have to stay up, it's part of our job, but why should you stand around here?"

No answer came from the shadows. The light of the lantern flickered briefly as if terrified by those waxy twisted faces, then abandoned them to the darkness.

"Good night," said Stres, entering the building and, lantern in hand, following his deputy down the staircase that led to the dungeon. The smell of mold choked him. He felt suddenly uneasy.

His aide pushed open the iron door of the dungeon and stood aside to let his chief pass. The prisoner was slumped on a pile of straw, head resting on his chained hands. Sensing a presence, he looked up. Stres could just make out his features in the gleam of the lantern. He seemed handsome, even marked as he was by the mud and the blows he had suffered. Stres's eyes were drawn involuntarily to the man's lips, and those human lips—cracked in the corners by fever, yet strangely alien to those shackles, those guards, those orders—suggested to Stres more than any other detail that he had before him the man who had made love to Doruntine.

"Who are you?" asked Stres, his voice icy.

The prisoner looked up. His expression, like his lips, seemed foreign to the setting. Seducer's eyes, Stres said to himself.

"I am a traveler, officer," the man answered. "An itinerant seller of icons. They arrested me. Why I don't know. I am very sick. I shall lodge a complaint."

He spoke a labored but correct Albanian. If he really was a seller of icons, he had apparently learned the language for his trade.

"Why did they arrest you?"

"Because of some woman I don't even know, whom I've never seen. A certain Doruntine. They told me I made a long journey on horseback, with her behind me, and they added I don't know what other foolishness as well."

"Did you really travel with a woman? More precisely, did you bring a woman here from far away?" Stres asked.

"No, officer, I did not. I have traveled with no woman at all, at least not in several years."

"About a month ago," said Stres.

"No. Absolutely not!"

"Think about it," said Stres.

"I don't have to think about it," said the shackled man in a sonorous voice. "I am sorry to see, officer, that you too apparently subscribe to this general foolishness. I am an honest man. I was arrested while lying on the roadside in agony. It's inhuman! To suffer like a dog and wake up in chains instead of finding help or care. It is truly insane!"

"I am no madman," said Stres. "As I think you will have occasion to find out."

"But what you're doing is pure madness," the man in shackles replied in the same stentorian voice. "At least accuse me of something plausible. Say that I stole something or killed someone. But don't come and tell me, You traveled on horseback with a woman. As if that was a crime! I would have done better to admit it from the outset, then you would all have been satisfied: yes, I traveled on horseback with a woman. And what of it? What's wrong with that? But I am an honest man, and if I did not say it, it is because I am not in the habit of lying. I intend to lodge a complaint about this wherever I can. I'll go to your prince himself. Higher still if need be, to Constantinople!"

Stres stared at him. The shackled man bore his scrutiny calmly.

"Well," said Stres, "be that as it may, once again I ask you the question you find so insane. This will be the last time. Think carefully before you answer. Did you bring a young woman named Doruntine Vranaj here from Bohemia or from any other far-off place?"

"No," the prisoner replied firmly.

"Wretch," said Stres, turning his eyes from the man. "Put him to the torture," he ordered.

The man's eyes widened in terror. He opened his mouth to speak or to scream, but Stres charged out of the dungeon. As he followed a guard carrying a lantern up the stairs, he quickened his pace so as not to hear the prisoner's cries.

A few minutes later he was on his way home, alone. The rain had stopped, but the path was dimpled with puddles. He let his boots splash in the water as he strode along absently, unseeing. It's dark, you see, he muttered to himself, repeating the words of the seller of icons.

He thought he heard a voice in the distance, but it was a barking that moved farther away and faded little by little, like circles on the water, in the expanse of the night.

It must be foggy, he thought, or the shadows would not be so deep.

He thought he heard that voice again, and even the muffled sound of footsteps. He started and looked back. Now he could make out the gleam of a lantern swaying in the distance, lighting the broken silhouette of a man in its wan glow. He stopped. The lantern and the splashing of the puddles, which seemed to rise up from a nightmare, were still quite far off when he first heard the voice. He cupped his hand to his ear, trying to make out the words. There were "uh's" and "eh's," but he heard nothing more distinct. When the man with the lantern had finally come closer, Stres called out:

"What is it?"

"He has confessed," the man answered, breathless. "He has confessed!"

He has confessed, Stres repeated. So those were the words that had sounded to him like "uh's" and "eh's." He has confessed!

Stres, still motionless, waited until the messenger reached him. He was breathing hard.

"God be praised, he has confessed," the messenger said again, brandishing his lantern as if to make his words more understandable. "Scarcely had he seen the instruments of torture when he broke down."

Stres looked at him numbly.

"Are you coming back? I'll light the way. Will you question him now?"

Stres did not answer. In fact, that was what the regulation called for. You were supposed to interrogate the prisoner immediately after his confession, while he was still exhausted, without giving him time to recover. And it was the middle of the night, the best time.

The man with the lantern stood two paces away, still panting.

I must not let him recover, Stres said to himself. Of course. Don't allow him even an instant of respite. Don't let him collect himself. That's right, he thought, that's exactly right as far as he's concerned, but what about me? Don't I too need to recover my strength?

And suddenly he realized that the interrogation of the prisoner might well be more trying for him than for the suspect.

"No," he said, "I won't interrogate him tonight. I need some rest." And he turned his back on the man with the lantern.

The next morning, when Stres went down to the cell with his aide, he detected what he thought was a guilty smile on the prisoner's face.

"Yes, truly I would have done better to confess from the start," he said before Stres could ask him a single question. "That's what I had thought to do in any case, for after all I have committed no crime, and no one has ever yet been condemned for traveling or wandering about in a woman's company. Had I told the truth from the beginning, I would have spared myself this torture, and instead of lying in this dungeon, I would have been at home, where my family is waiting for me. The problem is that once I found myself caught up in this maelstrom of lies—unwittingly, quite by chance—I couldn't extricate myself. For like a man who, after telling some small, inoffensive lie, sinks deeper and deeper instead of taking it back right away, so I too believed that I could escape this vexed affair by inventing things which, far from delivering me from my first lie, plunged me further into it. It was all the ruckus about this young woman's journey that got me into this mess. So let me repeat that if I did not confess at once it was only because when I realized what a furor this whole story had caused, and how deeply it had upset everyone, I suddenly felt like a child who has shifted some object the moving of which is a frightful crime in the eyes of the grownups. On the morning of that day—I'll tell you everything in detail in just a minute—when I saw that the arrival of this young woman had been so, so—how shall I put it?—so disturbing to everyone, especially when everyone suddenly started

134

running around so feverishly asking 'Who was she with?' and 'Who brought her back?', my instinct was to slip away, to get myself out of the whole affair, in which my role, after all, was in any event quite accidental. And that is what I tried to do. Anyway, now I'll tell you the whole story from the beginning. I think you want to know everything, in detail, isn't that right, officer?"

Stres stood as if frozen near the rough wooden table.

"I'm listening," he said. "Tell me everything you think you ought to."

The suspect seemed a little uneasy at Stres's indifferent air.

"I don't know, this is the first time I've ever been interrogated, but from what I've heard, the investigator is supposed to ask questions first, then the prisoner answers, isn't that how it works? But you. . . ."

"Tell me what you have to say," Stres said. "I'm listening."

The prisoner shifted on his pile of straw.

"Are your shackles bothering you?" Stres asked. "Do you want me to have them taken off?"

"Yes, if that's possible."

Stres motioned to his deputy to release him.

"Thank you," said the prisoner.

He seemed even less self-assured when his hands were freed, and he looked up at Stres once more, still hoping that he would be questioned. But once he realized that his hope was futile, he began speaking in a low voice, his earlier liveliness gone.

"As I told you yesterday, I am an itinerant seller of icons, and it was because of my trade that I happened to make the acquaintance of this young woman. I am from Malta, but I spend most of the year on the road in the Balkans and other parts of Europe. Please stop me if I'm giving you too much detail, for as I said, this is my first interrogation and I'm not sure of the rules. Anyway, I sell icons, and you can well imagine the taste women have for these objects. That was how I came to meet this woman Doruntine in Bohemia one day. She told me that she was a foreigner, originally from Albania, that she had married into a Bohemian family. When I mentioned that I had spent some time in her country, she could not contain her emotion. She said that I was the first person from there that she had met. She asked whether I had any news about what was happening there, whether some calamity had occurred, for none of her family had come to see her. I had heard talk of a war or a plague—in any case a scourge of some kind that had ravaged your country—and after telling her that, I added, hoping to set her mind at rest, that it had happened a long time ago, nearly three years before. Then she cried out, saying : 'But it is exactly three years since I have had any news! Oh woe is me! Surely something terrible must have happened!' Then, overcome, her voice broken by sobs, she told me that she had married a man from this land three years before, that her mother and brothers had not approved of her marrying so far away, but that one of her brothers, whose name was Constantine, had insisted on it. He had given his mother his word, his *bessa,* as you Albanians now call one's pledged word—though it was from her lips that I first heard the expression—promising to bring her daughter back from that far country whenever she wanted him to; that weeks and months had passed, and then years, but no one from her family had come to see her, not even Constantine, and she missed them so much she couldn't bear it, she felt so alone there among foreigners, and what with missing them so much and feeling so alone, she had begun to feel great anxiety that some catastrophe had happened at home. And since I had told her that there had in fact been a war or a plague, she was sure that something terrible had happened, that her forebodings were well founded. Then she said that she had been thinking of going to see her family herself, but she could not disobey her husband who, though he had promised to take her there, since her brothers seemed to have forsaken her, was too busy with his own affairs to undertake such a long journey.

"As I listened to her speak—in tears she looked even more beautiful—I was suddenly gripped by a desire for her so violent that without a moment's thought I said that if she agreed I could take her to her family myself. My trade has accustomed me to long journeys, and I told her that as simply as if I had offered to take her to the next town, but she thought the idea mad. It was only natural for it to seem insane to her at first, yet curiously, the passion with which she initially rejected my proposal gave me hope, for I had the impression that her protest was meant not so much to persuade me that the idea was really insane as to convince herself. The more she said, 'You're mad, and I am madder still for listening to you,' the more I felt my desire increase, along with my hope that she would yield. So on the next day, when after a sleepless night she told me—pale, her voice dull—that she did not see what she could say to her husband if she agreed to come with me, I told myself that I had won. I was convinced that the main thing was to set out alone with her on the roads of Europe. After that, God would provide! Nothing else seemed to matter. I suggested that we didn't have to tell him, for at bottom it was he who was forcing her to act in that way. Had she herself not told me that he had promised to take her to her mother, but that he was kept from doing so by his business? All she had to do, then, was to leave without telling him anything. But how can I, how can I, she asked feverishly. How can I explain it to him afterwards? Alone with a stranger! And she blushed. Of course not, I said, you cannot tell him that you made the journey with a stranger, God forbid! "Then what can I do?" she asked. And I told her: I've thought about it, and what you must do is leave him a letter saying that your brother came to fetch you in great haste, for misfortune has befallen your family. 'What misfortune?' she interrupted. 'You, stranger, you know what it is, but you don't want to tell me. Oh, my brother must be dead, otherwise he would have come to see me!'

"Two days passed and still she hesitated. I was afraid of being found out and tried to meet her secretly. My desire became uncontrollable. At last she agreed. It was a gloomy late afternoon when she came in haste to the crossroads where I had told her that I would wait for her one last time. I helped her to the crupper and we set off without a word. We rode for a long time, until we felt that we were far enough away that they would not be able to trace us. We spent the night in an out-of-the-way inn and set off again before dawn. I need hardly tell you that she was in a constant state of anxiety. I comforted her as well as I could, and we pressed on. We spent the second night in another inn even farther off the beaten track than the first, in a region I don't even know the name of. I'll spare you the details of my attempts to win her favors. Her pride, and especially her constant anxiety, held her back. But I used every means, from passionate entreaty to threats to abandon her, to leave her alone on the high plateaus of Europe. And so, on the fourth night she gave in. I was so drunk with passion, so giddy, that by the next morning I hardly knew where we were or where we were going. If I am giving useless detail, please stop me. We spent several strange days and nights. We slept in inns that we passed on the way, then we took up our journey again. We sold some of her jewels to pay our expenses. I wanted the journey to last as long as possible, but she was impatient. The closer we came to the Albanian border, the greater was her anxiety. What could have happened there? she asked from time to time. What of that war, that plague? We asked often at the inns, but received only evasive answers. There had indeed been talk of great conflict in Albanian territory, but the reports differed about when it had happened. Some said it had not been war, but plague; others held that the disease had not stricken Albania, but some more distant land. Meanwhile, as we neared the Albanian border, the answers grew more definite. Without telling her, I tried to find out more while she rested at the inns. Here everyone knew that war and plague had allied themselves, and had decimated the men of Albania. Once we were in the country's northern principalities, we tried to avoid the major roads and inns, traveling mostly by night. We had now reached the principalities neighboring her own, and she insisted that we do nothing to call attention to ourselves. We cut across fallow fields, often leaving the roads altogether. We made love wherever we could. In one of the few inns in which we were forced to take shelter by bad weather, I learned the terrible truth about her brothers. Everyone was talking about the great sorrow that had befallen that illustrious house. All her brothers were dead, Constantine among them. The innkeeper knew the whole story. I began to fear that she would be recognized. As we came closer to her home, we strained our wits to find some acceptable explanation for her arrival. Believing her brothers still alive, she was more frightened than she need have been, whereas for me, knowing the truth as I did, things seemed simpler. In any event, it was easier to account to an old woman stunned by misfortune than to nine brothers.

"She was beside herself in her anxiety about what she could say to her brothers and her mother to explain her arrival. What would she answer when they asked her, 'Who brought you back?' Would she tell the truth? Would she lie? And if so what would she say?

"So I found myself compelled to tell her a part of the truth; that is, of the terrible misfortune. I gave her to understand that her brother Constantine, the one who had promised to bring her back, had died, together with some of his brothers.

"You can well imagine that she went mad with grief, but neither the fatigue of the journey nor her sorrow lessened her worry over the explanation she would have to give for her sudden arrival. It was I who had the idea of explaining her journey in terms of some supernatural intervention. Though I racked my brain, I could find no better explanation. 'There is no other way,' I told her. 'You have to repeat the lie you've already used with your husband. You'll say that Constantine brought you back.' 'But I was able to lie to my husband,' she replied, 'because he believed my brother was still alive. How can I say the same thing about someone they know is dead?' 'But it'll be even easier,' I told her, 'just because he isn't alive. You'll say that it was your brother who brought you, and they can take it any way they like. What I mean is, they have only to imagine that it was his ghost who brought you back. After all, didn't he promise that, dead or alive, he would fetch you? Everyone knows the exact words of his promise, and they will believe you.'

"Since I knew that her mother alone was still alive, I found the matter quite simple, but she, thinking as she did that at least half of her brothers were alive, scarcely hoped to be believed. But like it or not, she had to yield to my reasoning. There was no other way. We had no time to think of a more plausible explanation, and in any case neither of us was thinking clearly by then.

"And so, the last night came, the night of October eleventh if I am not mistaken, when, slipping through the darkness like ghosts, we came up to the house. I won't try to tell you about her state of mind—I couldn't describe it. It was past midnight. As we had decided, I stood out of sight, hiding in the half-darkness as she went toward the door. But she was in no condition to walk. So I had to lead her to the door where, her hand trembling, she knocked, or more accurately she rested her hand on the knocker, for it was I in fact who moved her hand, cold as a corpse's. I wanted to run off at once, but she was terrified, and wouldn't let go of me. In order to calm her, I stroked her hair with my other hand one last time, but at that instant, God be praised, she not only let go, but pushed me away in terror. I heard the old woman's voice from behind the door: 'Who is it?', then her answer: 'Open, Mother, it's me, Doruntine,' then the old woman's voice again: 'What did you say?' I had moved away and could not hear the other words clearly, the more so because they were increasingly faint and interrupted with exclamations.

"I made my way back to the highway, to the place where I had left my horse and, mounting, I wandered awhile looking for shelter for the night. We had agreed to meet secretly in two days, but at that point I knew that I would never see her again. The next day and in the days that followed, as I saw the turmoil caused by her arrival, I became convinced not only that I would never see her again but that I had better leave these parts as quickly as possible. I had in the meantime heard of the orders you had issued, and was sure that I was guilty of something impious which, however unaware of it I may have been, might cost me dear indeed. I wanted to slip away as quickly as possible, but how? All the inns, all the relay stations, had been alerted to arrest me on sight. At first I thought of turning myself in and confessing: yes, it was I who brought this woman back, forgive me if I did something wrong, but if I did, it was without realizing it. Then I changed my mind. Why take such a risk? With a bit of skill I could evade the traps that were set for me and be quit of the whole affair. Yet I had a premonition that the honeymoon I had spent with that young woman would turn out to be deadly poison. I moved about very cautiously, far from the roads and inns, and mostly by night. I thought that if I could cross the border of your principality I would be out of danger. I didn't know that the neighboring principalities and counties had also been notified. And that's how I came to grief. I caught a cold while fording a stream by the baneful name of the Wicked Uyan—I think that was the name—and I am not quite sure what happened to me next. I was burning with fever, and I remember nothing until I came to and found myself bound hand and foot in an inn. And that's it, Captain. I don't know if I have explained everything properly, but you can ask me any detail at all, and I'll tell you everything. I'm sorry that I didn't behave as I should have from the very beginning, but I hope you'll understand my situation. I'll do everything I can to make amends by answering all your questions honestly."

At last he fell silent, and he sat unblinking under Stres's inspection. His mouth was dry, but he dared not ask for water. Stres stared at him for a long moment. Then, as he opened his mouth to speak, a smile crossed his face like a flash of lightning.

"Is that the truth?" Stres asked.

"Yes, Captain. The whole truth."

"Oh?"

"Yes. The whole truth, Captain."

Stres rose and, his neck stiff as a board, slowly turned his head toward his deputy and the two guards.

"Put him to the torture," he ordered.

Not only the prisoner, but the three other men as well, stiffened in astonishment.

"Torture?" asked his deputy, as though afraid he had misunderstood.

"Yes," said, Stres, his tone icy. "Torture. And don't look at me like that. I know what I'm doing."

He turned on his heels, but at that instant, behind him, the prisoner began to scream:

"Captain, no! No! My God, what is this? Why, why?"

Stres climbed the stairs quickly, but he still heard the clanking of the chains with which they secured the prisoner, and his cries as well, which were no less poignant for being muffled.

Stres returned to his office, took up a pencil, and began drafting a report for the prince's chancellery:

Report on the arrest of the man who brought back Doruntine Vranaj

Last night Captain Stanish of the border detachment delivered to me the man suspected of having brought Doruntine back. In the first interrogation he admitted nothing and denied even knowing a woman by that name, much less having traveled with her. Then, under the threat of torture, he confessed everything, finally throwing light on the mystery of this affair. The events seem to have happened in this manner: At the end of September of this year the man, finding himself in Bohemia in the course of his peregrinations as a seller of icons, made the acquaintance of D.V. and hearing her express her despair at having had no news of her family, promised to lead her to her parents' home. He persuaded her to lie to her husband and to write him a letter saying that she had left with her brother Constantine. The two of them then left Bohemia. On the way he managed to seduce her. At the conclusion of this trying journey, after revealing to her that her brother Constantine was long dead and finding no other lie with which to justify the journey she had just made with a stranger, he persuaded her to tell her mother that she had been brought back by the ghost of her dead brother, who had thereby fulfilled the promise he had made while he was alive. Subsequently, taking fright, he tried to flee unnoticed and was finally arrested, under circumstances that are well known to you, in the neighboring county, in an establishment called the Inn of the Two Roberts. He is now being held, on my orders, in complete isolation. I

146

await your instructions on the measures to be taken in this case.

Captain Stres

Of the torture he had ordered inflicted on the prisoner down below in the basement Stres said not a word. He closed the envelope carefully, sealed it, and instructed a courier to set out at once to deliver it to the capital of the principality. A more or less identical letter was sent to the archbishop at the Monastery of the Three Crosses, with a notice asking that it be forwarded to him in the capital if necessary.

CHAPTER VI

*I*t had started snowing again, but this snow was different from the last, somehow closer to the world of men. That which was meant to be whitened was whitened, and that which was fated to stay dark remained so. The first icicles hung from the eves, some of the rivulets had frozen as usual, and the layer of ice was just strong enough to support the weight of the birds. It soon appeared that this would be one of those winters the earth could live with.

Under roofs weighed down by their heavy burden the people talked of Doruntine. By now every-

149

one knew of the arrest of the man who had brought her back, and though they had heard only bits and pieces of the tale he had told, that was enough to cover all the world with words, just as a handful of wheat can sow a field.

Many were the messengers who fanned out from the capital through the province during those days, while others, equally numerous, were dispatched from the province to the capital. It was said that a great assembly was being prepared, at which all the rumors and agitation aroused by the alleged resurrection of one of the Vranaj brothers would be laid to rest once and for all. Stres was said to be preparing a detailed report to be presented at that meeting. He had kept the prisoner in isolation, his whereabouts unknown, safe from prying eyes and ears.

Those bits and pieces of the prisoner's confession that had somehow leaked out were now spreading far and wide, carried by word of mouth on puffs of mist in the winter air and borne by carriage from road to road and inn to inn. People traveled less than usual because of the cold, but strangely, the rumors spread just as fast as they would have in more clement weather. It was as if, hardened to crystalline brilliance by the winter frost, they flowed more surely than the rumors of summer, for they were unimpeded by damp and suffocating heat, by the numbing of minds and the jangling of nerves. But that did not prevent them from changing daily as they spread, from swelling, from becoming lighter or darker. And as if all were not enough, there were still those who said, "Just wait, even stranger things will come." Others, drifting off, would simply sigh, "What next, Lord, what next?"

Everyone awaited the great assembly at which the whole affair would be sifted in minute detail. The arrival of many nobles from all the principalities of Albania was announced. Rumor had it that the prince himself would attend. Other voices whispered that high church dignitaries from Byzantium would participate, while others, less numerous, even suggested that the Patriarch himself would come in person.

In fact, contrary to what might have been expected, echoes of the Doruntine affair had spread far indeed. The news had even reached Constantinople, capital of the Orthodox religion, and no one was unaware that such things were never pardoned in that city. The highest ecclesiastical authorities were worried, people said. The Emperor himself had been apprised of the incident, which had given him sleepless nights. The issue had proven far more ticklish than it had seemed at first. It was not a simple case of a ghostly apparition, nor even one of those typical calumnies that the Church had always punished with the stake and always would. No, this was far more serious, something that, may God protect us, was shaking the Orthodox religion to its foundations. It concerned the coming of a new messiah—in God's name, lower your voice!—yes, a new messiah, for one man alone had been able to rise from his grave, and that was Jesus Christ, and whosoever affirmed this new resurrection was thereby guilty of an unpardonable sacrilege: belief in a new resurrection, which was tantamount to admitting that there could be two Jesus Christs, for if one believed that someone today had succeeded in doing what Jesus had done in His time, then it was but one small step to admitting—may God preserve us!—that this someone else might be His rival.

Not for nothing had Rome, in its hostility, paid the most careful attention to the development of the case. The Catholic monks had surely outdone themselves in propagating this fable of Constantine's resurrection, thereby attempting to deal the Orthodox religion a mortal blow by accusing it of a monstrous heresy leading to dual Christs. Things had gotten so tense that there was now talk of a universal war of religion. Some even hinted that the impostor who had brought Doruntine back was himself an agent of the Roman Church entrusted with just that mission. Others went further still, claiming that Doruntine herself had fallen into Catholic clutches and had agreed to do their bidding. O great God above, people intoned, may it not be our lot to hear such things! That is how entangled the case had become. But the Orthodox

Church of Byzantium, which had spared neither patriarchs nor emperors for infractions of this magnitude, had finally taken the matter in hand and would clear it all up soon enough. The enemies of the Church would be utterly routed.

So said some. Others shook their heads. Not because they disagreed, but because they suspected that the rumor of Constantine's return from the grave might well have been generated not by the intrigues and rivalry of the world's two major religions but by one of those mysterious disturbances which, like a wicked wind, periodically plagues the minds of men, robbing them of judgment, numbing them, and driving them thus dazed and blinded beyond life and death. For life and death, as they saw it, enveloped man in endless successive concentric layers, so that just as there was death within life, so death ought to contain life, which in turn contained death; or perhaps life, itself enveloped in death, harbored death in turn, and so on to infinity. Enough, objected the first group: forget the hairsplitting ratiocination, just say what you mean. The others then sought to explain their point of view more clearly, talking fast lest a mist descend upon their reasoning once more. This alleged resurrection of Constantine, they said, was in no sense real, and the hoax had been born not at that churchyard grave but in the minds of the people, who, it seemed, had been somehow gripped by a powerful yearning to spin this tale of the mingling of life and death, just as they are sometimes gripped by collective madness. This yearning had cropped up in scattered places, with one, then with another; it had infected them all, so as to turn, at last—abomination of abominations—into a common desire of the quick and the dead to give themselves over to this collective outburst. Short-sighted as they were, people gave no real thought to the abomination they had wrought, for though it is true that everyone feels the urge to see their dead once more, that longing is ephemeral, always arising after some time of turmoil (something stopped me from kissing him, Doruntine had said). If the dead ever really came back and sat before us big as life, you'd see just how terrifying it would be. You think it's difficult to get along with a nonagenarian? Well, imagine dealing with a 900-year-old! Constantine's presence, too, like that of any other dead man returned to the land of the living, would be welcome for no more than the briefest lapse of time (you go on, I have something to do at the church), for his dead life's proper place was in the grave. They say there was a time when dead and living, men and gods, all lived together and sometimes even intermarried, engendering hybrid creatures. But that was an era of barbarism that would never return.

Others listened to these morbid words but preferred to look at matters more simply. If this was all some yearning for resurrection, they said, why bother trying to decide whether it was good or ill? God, after all, would set the date of the Apocalypse, and none save Him was entitled to pass judgment on the matter, and still less to decree its advent. But that, others replied, is exactly what's wrong with this rumor of Constantine's resurrection. The alleged resurrection is taken as a sign that the Apocalypse could occur without an order from the Lord. And the Roman Church accuses ours of having sanctioned this travesty. Now, however, everything will be put right. The Church of Byzantium will not be found wanting. Stres had finally unmasked the great hoax, and the whole country—nay, the whole world, from Rome to Constantinople—would soon learn the truth. Stres would surely be awarded high honors for his achievement.

The light in his window was the last to go out each night. He must be preparing his report. Who can say what we're going to find out, everyone repeated.

All the talk was of Doruntine's life. Only the mourners had changed nothing in their ritual. On the day of the dead, as people made the traditional visits to the graves of their relatives, these women mourned the Vranaj with the very same songs they had sung before:

> Constantine, may evil strike you!
> What has become of your promise,
> Have you buried it with you?

155

Stres listened to all the talk with an enigmatic smile. For some time now he had been looking pale.

"What exactly does the *bessa* mean to you?" he would ask of Constantine's companions—recently he had found pleasure in their company.

The young men looked at one another. There were four of them: Shpëndë, Milosao, and the two Radhen boys. Stres met them nearly every afternoon at the New Inn, where they used to pass the time when Constantine was alive. People shook their heads in wonder when they saw Stres with them. Some said that he frequented them as a matter of official duty. Others maintained that he was just killing time. He has finished his report, they said, and now he's resting. Others simply shrugged. Who knows why he spends his time with them? He's deep as a well, that Stres. You can never guess why he does one thing rather than another.

"So, what does *bessa* mean to you? Or rather, what did it mean to him, to Constantine?"

No one had been more deeply moved by Constantine's death than these four young men. He had been more than a brother to them, and even now, three years after his death, so strong was his presence in their words and thoughts that many people, half-seriously, half-jokingly, called them "Constantine's disciples." They looked at one another again. Why was Stres asking them this question?

They had not accepted the captain's company

with good grace. Even when Constantine was alive they had been cool towards him, but recently, as Stres labored to unravel the mystery of Doruntine's return, the chill had turned icy, bordering on hostility. Stres's first efforts to win them over had run up against that wall. But later, surprisingly, their attitude had changed completely and they accepted the captain's presence. Young people today are not stupid, was the popular comment at church on Sunday; they know what they're doing.

"It's a term that was used in olden days," Stres went on, "but the meaning attached to it in our own day seems to me more or less new. It has come up more than once in trial proceedings."

They sat there, thoughtful. During their many afternoons and evenings with Constantine, so different from the morose sessions that were now their lot, they had discussed many subjects with great passion, but the *bessa* had always been their favorite topic. And for good reason too: it was a sort of fulcrum, the theme on which all the rest was based.

They had begun to weigh their words with greater care after the bishop issued warnings to all their families. But that was before Constantine's death. What would they do now that the man they had loved so much was gone? Stres seemed to be familiar with their ideas already; that being the case, all he really had to do was sit and listen. After all, they were not afraid to express their views. On the contrary, given the opportunity they were prepared to proclaim them quite openly. What they feared was that their views might be distorted.

"What did Constantine think about the *bessa*?" said Milosao, repeating Stres's question. "It was part of his more general ideas. It would be difficult to explain it without showing its connection with his other convictions."

And they set about explaining everything to him in detail. Constantine, as the captain must surely know, was an oppositionist, a dissident, as were they, come to that. He was opposed to existing laws, institutions, decrees, prisons, police, and courts, which he considered no more than a pack of coercive rules raining down on man from the outside like hail. He believed that these laws ought to be abolished and replaced by inner laws arising from within man himself. By this he did not mean purely spiritual standards dependent on conscience alone, for he was no naive dreamer who assumed that humanity could be ruled solely by conscience. He believed in something far more tangible, something the seeds of which he had detected scattered here and there in Albanian life in recent times, something he said should be nurtured, encouraged to blossom into a whole system. In this system there would be no further need for written laws, courts, jails, or police. This new order, of course, would not be wholly free of tragedy, of killing and violence, but man himself would judge his neighbor and be judged by him quite apart from any rigid judicial structure. He would kill or be executed, he would imprison himself or leave prison, when he thought it appropriate.

"But how could such an order be achieved?" asked Stres. Didn't it still come down to conscience in the end, and did not they themselves consider it merely a dream?

They replied that in this new world, existing institutions would have been replaced by others, invisible, not material, but not at all chimerical nor idyllic. In fact they would be rather bleak and tragic, and therefore as weighty as the old ones, if not more so. Except that they would lie within man, not in the form of remorse or some similar sentiment, but as a well-defined ideal, a faith, an order understood and accepted by everyone, but realized within each individual, not secret but revealed for all the world to see, as if man's breast were transparent and his greatness or anguish, his pain, his tragedy, his decisions and doubts, were visible for all to see. Such would be the axes of an order of this kind. The *bessa* was one of them, perhaps the principal one.

It was still very rare: delicate, like a wild flower needing tender care, its shape as yet undefined. To illustrate their thesis, they reminded Stres of an incident that had occurred some years before, when Constantine was still alive. In a village not far off, a man had killed his guest. Stres had heard talk of the case. It was then that the expression "He violated the *bessa*" had been used. Everyone in the village, young and old, had been deeply shaken by the event. Together they decided that no such disgrace would ever befall them again. In fact they went further still, decreeing that anyone, known or unknown, who entered the territory of their village would stand under the protection of the *bessa* and would thereby be declared a friend and be protected as such, that the doors of the village would be opened to anyone, at any hour of night or day, and that any passer-by must be given food, and his safety assured. In the marketplace of the capital they were the butt of jokes. Anyone want a free meal? Just head for that village and knock on any door; talk about consideration, they'll escort you to the village border as if you were a bishop. But the villagers, ignoring the mockery, went even further. They requested—and received—the prince's permission to punish those who violated the *bessa*. No one guilty of that offense could leave the territory of the village alive. Another village, quite far from the first, asked the prince to grant them the same right, but their lord, fearing the spread of the practice, refused. That was what the *bessa* meant. That was how Constantine saw it. He considered the *bessa* a bond linking all that was sublime, and he felt that once it and other similar laws had spread and held sway in every aspect of life, then external laws, with their corresponding institutions, would be

160

shed naturally, just as a snake sloughs off its old skin.

Thus spoke Constantine on those memorable afternoons they used to pass at the New Inn. As for myself, he said, I shall give my mother my *bessa* to bring Doruntine back to her from her husband's home whenever she desires. And whatever happens—if I am lying on my deathbed, if I have but one hand or one leg, if I have lost my sight, even if—I will never break that promise.

"Even if. . . .?" Stres repeated. "Tell me, Milosao, don't you think he meant 'even if I'm dead'?"

"Perhaps," the young man answered absently, looking away.

"But how can you account for that?" Stres asked. "He was an intelligent man, he didn't believe in ghosts. I have a report from the bishop stating that at Easter you and he laughed at people's faith in the resurrection of Christ. So how could he have believed in his own resurrection?"

They looked at one another, each suppressing a smile.

"You are right, Captain, so long as you are speaking of the present world, the existing world. But you must not forget that he, that all of us, in our words and thoughts, had in mind another world, one with a new dimension, a world in which the *bessa* reigned supreme. In that world

161

everything would be different."

"Nevertheless, you live in our world, in this existing world," said Stres.

"Yes. But a part of our being, perhaps the best, lies in the other."

"In the other," he repeated softly. Now it was he who suppressed a smile.

They took no notice of it, or pretended not to, and went on discussing Constantine's other ideas, the reasons why he held that this reorganization of life in Albania was necessary. These had to do with the great storms he saw looming on the horizon and with Albania's location, caught in a vise between the religions of Rome and Byzantium, between two worlds, West and East. Their clash would inevitably bring appalling turmoil, and Albania would have to find new ways to defend itself. It had to create structures more stable than "external" laws and institutions, structures eternal and universal, lying within man himself, inviolable and invisible and therefore indestructible. In short, Albania had to change its laws, its administration, its prisons, its courts and all the rest, had to fashion them so that they could be severed from the outside world and anchored within men themselves as the tempest drew near. It had to do this or it would be wiped from the face of the earth. Thus spoke Constantine. And he held that this new organization would begin with the *bessa*.

"Then of course," Stres said, "Constantine's own

default, the violation of his promise, was all the more serious and inadmissible, was it not?"

"Oh yes, certainly. Especially after his mother's curse. Except for one thing, Captain Stres: there was no default. He kept his promise in the end. Somewhat belatedly, of course, but he had a good enough reason for being late: he was dead. In the end he kept his word in spite of everything."

"But he was not the one who brought Doruntine back," said Stres. "You know that as well as I do."

"For you, perhaps, it wasn't him. We see it differently."

"Truth is the same for all. Almost anyone could have brought Doruntine here, but certainly not he."

"Nevertheless, it was he who brought her back."

"So you believe in resurrection?"

"That's secondary. It has nothing to do with the heart of the matter."

"Just the same, if you don't accept the resurrection of the dead, how can you persist in claiming that he made that journey with his sister?"

"But that is of no importance, Captain Stres. That is completely secondary. The essential thing is that it was he who brought Doruntine here."

"Maybe it's this business about two worlds that prevents us from understanding one another," Stres said. "What is a lie in one may be the truth in the other, is that the idea?"

"Perhaps. Perhaps."

Meanwhile, the country seethed as it awaited the great assembly. Words, calculations, forebodings, and news fluttered in the wind like yellowing leaves before a storm, falling to earth only to be raised anew. Messengers plied to and fro between the capital and the provinces. No one was sure just when the meeting would take place, but everyone knew that it would not be long.

CHAPTER VII

*I*t was in an inner courtyard of the Old Monastery, large enough to hold some two thousand people, that the great assembly was to be held. Carpenters spent several days setting up wooden grandstands for the guests and a platform from which Stres would speak. Canvas covers were strung up in case of rain.

The meeting was to take place on the first Sunday in December, but by mid-week most of the region's inns were full, not only those closest to the Old Monastery, but also the ones along the highway. Guests, clergy and laymen alike, poured in from the four corners of the principality and from neighboring principalities, dukedoms, and counties. Visitors were expected from the farthest principalities, and envoys from the Holy Patriarchate in the Empire's capital.

As they watched the carriages parade down the highway—most of their doors decorated with coats of arms, the passengers dressed in gaudy clothes often embroidered with the same coats of arms as the one on their coaches—the people, chatting with one another, learned more in those few days about princely courts, ceremonies, dignitaries, and religious and secular hierarchies than they had in their whole lifetime. It was only then that they came to realize the full import, the truly enormous significance, of this whole affair, which at first, on that night of October eleventh, had been considered simply a ghost story. On the eve of the assembly, Stres went to the Old Monastery to inspect the meeting place. Their preparations complete, the carpenters had gathered up their tools and gone. A fine rain had dampened the exposed tiers of seats. Stres mounted the platform from which he was to speak and stood there a moment, eyes fixed on the empty stands.

He stared at them for a long time, then suddenly turned his head sharply right and left, as though someone had called him or he had heard shouts. The hint of a bitter smile crossed his face; then, with long strides, he walked away.

Finally the long-awaited day dawned. It was cold, one of those days that seems all the more icy when you realize it's Sunday. The high clouds were motionless, as if moored to the heavens. From early morning the monastery's inner courtyard was packed with spectators—except for the stands reserved for high-ranking officials and guests from other principalities and Constantinople—and the innumerable latecomers, hoping to be able to hear something, had no choice but to assemble outside in the empty field that ringed the walls. They had at all costs to learn what was said at the gathering, and quickly, for they formed the first circle the news must reach so that it might spread in waves throughout the world.

Bundled up in gray goatskins to protect themselves from the cold and the rain, they watched the arrival of the endless procession of horses and carriages from which the invited guests descended. In the courtyard the stands were gradually filling up. Last to take their seats were the personal envoy of the prince, the delegates from Byzantium (accompanied by the archbishop of the principality), and Stres, dressed in his black uniform with the deer antler insignia, looking taller, but also paler, than usual.

The archbishop left the group of guests and walked toward the platform, apparently to open the meeting. Many took up the hissing "ssh" as silence gradually settled over the great courtyard.

Only when it had become almost complete was that silence broken by a rumbling that had hitherto been inaudible. It was the noise of the crowd outside the monastery walls.

The archbishop tried to speak in a strong, sonorous voice, but without the cathedral cupola he could not be truly resounding. He seemed annoyed at the weakness of his voice and cleared his throat, but its timbre was muffled mercilessly by the vastness of the courtyard whose walls, had they not been so low, might perhaps have given resonance and volume to his eloquence. But the prelate spoke on nonetheless. He briefly mentioned the purpose of this enlarged meeting, convoked to shed light upon the great hoax that had so regrettably been born in this village with "someone's alleged return from the grave and his journey with some living woman." (His tone as he spoke the words *someone's* and *some* gave his audience to understand that he disdained to cite the names of Constantine and Doruntine.) He mentioned the spread of this hoax throughout the principality, beyond its borders, and indeed even beyond the confines of Albania; he suggested what unimaginable catastrophes could result if such heresies were permitted to spread freely. And finally he noted the efforts by the Church of Rome to exploit the heresy, using it against the Holy Byzantine Church, as well as the measures taken by the latter to unmask the imposture.

"And now," he concluded, "I yield the platform to Captain Stres, who was entrusted with the investigation of this matter and who will now present a detailed report on all aspects of it. He will explain to you, step by step, how the hoax was conceived; he will tell you who was behind the story of the dead man returned from the grave, what the pretended journey of the sister with her dead brother really was, what happened afterwards, and how the truth was brought to light."

A deep rumbling drowned out his final words as Stres rose from his seat and headed for the platform.

He raised his head, looked out at the crowd, and waited for the first layer of silence to fall over it once more. He spoke his first words in a voice that seemed very soft. Little by little, as the crowd's silence grew deeper, it gained strength. In chronological order he set out the events of the night of October eleventh and after; he recalled Doruntine's arrival, her claim to have returned in the company of her dead brother, and his own initial suspicions: that an impostor had deceived Doruntine, that Doruntine herself had lied both to her mother and to him, that the young woman and her partner had hatched the hoax in concert, or even that it was no more than a belated vendetta of some kind, a settling of accounts or struggle for succession. He then reviewed the measures taken to discover the truth, the research into the family archives, the checks on the inns and relay stations, and finally the failure of all these various efforts to shed any light at all on the mystery. Then he recalled the spread of the first rumors, mentioning the mourners, his suspicion that Doruntine had gone mad and that the trip with her brother was no more than the product of a diseased imagination. But at that point, he continued, the arrival of two members of the husband's family had confirmed that the journey had really occurred and that the horseman who had taken Doruntine up behind him had been seen. Stres then described the fresh measures that he and other officials of the principality had been compelled to take in their effort to solve the mystery, measures that led at length to the capture of the impostor—the man who had played the role of the dead brother—at the Inn of the Two Roberts in the next county.

"I interrogated him myself," Stres continued. "At first he denied knowing Doruntine. In fact he denied everything, and it was only when I ordered him put to the torture that he confessed. Here, according to him, is what really happened."

Stres then recounted the prisoner's confession. His every word brought murmurs of relief from the crowd. It was as if they had all been yearning for this bleak story, hitherto so macabre, to be freshened by the gentle breeze of the itinerant merchant's tale of romantic adventure. The rippling murmur breached the monastery walls and spread into the field beyond, just as silence, shuddering, and terror in turn had spread before.

"So much, then, for what the prisoner stated," Stres said, raising his voice. He paused for a moment, waiting for silence. "So much, then," he repeated, "for what the prisoner stated. It was midnight."

The silence grew deeper, but the murmur rising from the most distant rows, and especially from outside the walls, was still audible.

"It was midnight when he finished his account, and it was then that I—"

Here he paused again, in one final effort to unroll the carpet of silence as far as possible.

"Then, to the astonishment of my aides, I ordered him put to the torture again."

A sulfurous light seemed to glow in Stres's eyes. He gazed for a moment at those silent faces, at the darkened features of the people in the grandstands, and spoke again only when he was convinced that he had wrung the very last reserves of silence from the crowd.

"If I had him put to the torture again, it was because I doubted the truth of his tale."

Silence still reigned, but Stres thought he felt what could have been a mild earthquake. Now! he said to himself, intoxicated, now! Bring it all down!

"He resisted the torture for a week. Then, on the

eighth day, he confessed the truth at last. That is to say, he admitted that everything he had said until then had been nothing but lies."

The earthquake, which he had been the first to sense, had now in fact begun: its roar was rising, a muffled thunder, out of phase, of course, like any earthquake, but powerful nonetheless. A lightning glance to his right showed all was still mute there. But those frozen faces in the grandstands had suddenly clouded over.

"It was nothing but a tissue of lies from start to finish," Stres continued, surprised that he had not been interrupted. "The man had never met Doruntine, had never spoken to her, had neither traveled with her nor made love to her, any more than he had brought her back on the night of October eleventh. He had been paid to perpetrate the hoax."

Stres raised his head, waiting for something that he himself could not have defined.

"Yes," he went on, "paid. He himself confessed it, paid by persons whose names I shall not mention here."

He paused briefly once again. What reigned around him now resembled strangulation more than silence.

"At first," Stres went on, "when this impostor denied knowing Doruntine, he played his role to perfection, and he did equally well afterward, when he affirmed that in fact he had brought her back. But just as great impostors often betray themselves in small details, so he gave himself away with a trifle. Thus this impostor, this imaginary companion of Doruntine—"

"Then who brought the woman back?" shouted the archbishop from his seat. "The dead man?"

Stres turned toward him.

"Who brought Doruntine back? I will answer you on that very point, for I was in charge of this case. Be patient, Your Eminence, be patient, noble sirs!"

Stres took a deep breath. So many hundreds of lungs swelled along with his that he felt as if all the air about them had been set in motion. Once again he glanced slowly across the packed courtyard to the steps of the stands at the foot of which stood the guards, their arms crossed.

"I expected that question," said Stres, "and am therefore prepared to answer it." He paused again.

"Yes, I have prepared myself with the greatest care to answer it. The painstaking investigation I conducted is now closed, my file complete, my conviction unshakable. I am ready, noble sirs, to answer the question: Who brought Doruntine back?"

Stres allows yet another brief moment of silence, during which he glanced in all directions as if seeking to convey the truth with his eyes before expressing it with his voice.

"Doruntine," he said, "was in fact brought back by Constantine."

Stres stiffened, expecting some sound—laughter, jeers, shouts, an uproar of some kind, even a challenging cry: "But for two months you've been trying to convince us of the contrary!" Nothing of the kind came from the crowd.

"Yes, Doruntine was brought back by Constantine," he repeated as if he feared that he had been misunderstood. But the silence continued and he thought that that silence was perhaps excessive. It is all so trying, he sighed in his confusion. But then he felt an inspiration so powerful that it pained his chest, and the words poured out.

"Just as I promised you, noble sirs, and you, honored guests, I will explain everything. All I ask is that you have the patience to hear me out."

At that moment Stres's only concern was to keep his mind clear. For the time being he asked for nothing more.

"You have all heard," he began, "some of you before setting out for this gathering, others on your way here or upon your arrival, of the strange marriage of Doruntine Vranaj, the marriage that lies at the root of this whole affair. You are all aware, I imagine, that this far-off marriage, the first concluded with a man from so distant a country, would never have taken place if Constantine, one of the bride's brothers, had not given his mother his word that he would bring Doruntine back to her whenever she desired her daughter's presence, on occasions of joy or sorrow. You also know that not long

174

after the wedding the Vranaj, like all of Albania, were stricken with unspeakable grief. Yet no one brought Doruntine back, for he who had promised to do so was dead. You are aware of the curse the Lady Mother uttered against her son for his violation of the *bessa,* and you know that three weeks after that curse was spoken, Doruntine at last appeared at the family home. That is why I now affirm, and reaffirm, that it was none other than her brother Constantine, in accordance with his oath, his *bessa,* who brought Doruntine back. There is no explanation for that journey, nor could there be. It matters little whether or not Constantine returned from the grave to accomplish his mission, just as it matters little who was the horseman who set out on that black night or what horse he saddled, whose hands held the reins, whose feet pressed against the stirrups, whose hair was matted with the highway dust. Each of us has a part in that journey, for it is here among us that Constantine's *bessa* germinated, and that is what brought Doruntine back. Therefore, to be more exact I would have to say that it was all of us—you, me, our dead lying there in the graveyard close by the church—who, through Constantine, brought Doruntine back."

Stres swallowed.

"Noble sirs, I have not yet finished. I would like to tell you—and most of all to tell our guests from distant lands—just what this sublime power is that is capable of bending the laws of death."

175

Stres paused again. His throat felt dry and he found it hard to form his words. But he kept speaking just the same. He spoke of the *bessa,* of its spread among the Albanians. As he spoke he saw someone in the crowd coming toward him, holding what seemed to be a heavy object, perhaps a stone. Now it begins, he said to himself, his elbow brushing the pommel of his sword beneath his cloak. But when the man had come near, Stres saw that it was one of the Radhen boys, and that he carried not a stone to strike him with, but a small pitcher.

Stres smiled, took the pitcher and drank.

"And now," he went on, "let me try to explain why this new moral law was born and is now spreading among us."

He spoke briefly of the gravity of the world situation, of the troubled future, heavy with dark clouds, that now loomed because of the friction between great empires and religions; he spoke of the plots, the trickery, the faithlessness that flourished far and wide, and of Albania's position in the midst of that sea of storms and raging waves.

"Any people in danger," he continued, "hones the tools of its defense and, what is more important, it forges new ones. It would be short-sighted indeed not to realize that Albania faces great upheavals. Sooner or later they will reach its borders, if they have not already done so. So the question is this: in these new conditions of the worsening of the general atmosphere in the world, in this time of trial, of crime and hateful treachery, who should the Albanian be? What face shall he show the world? Shall he espouse the evil or stand against it? Shall he disfigure himself, changing his features to suit the masks of the age, seeking thus to assure his survival, or shall he keep his countenance unchanged at the risk of bringing upon himself the wrath of the age? Albania's time of trial is near, the hour of choice between these two faces. And if the people of Albania, deep within themselves, have begun to fashion institutions as sublime as the *bessa,* that shows us that Albania is making its choice. It was to carry that message to Albania and to the world beyond that Constantine rose from his grave."

Once more Stres's glance embraced the numberless crowd that stretched before him, then the stands to his right and left.

"But it is not easy to accept this message," he went on. "It will require great sacrifices by successive generations. Its burden will be heavier than the cross of Christ. And now that I have come to the end of what I had to tell you"—and here Stres turned to the stands where the envoys of the prince were seated—"I would like to add that, since my words are at variance with my duties, or at least are at variance with them *for the moment,* I now resign my post."

He raised his right hand to the white-antler insignia sewn to the left side of his cloak and, pulling sharply, ripped it off and let it fall to the ground.

Without another word he descended the wooden stairway and, his head high, walked through the crowd, which parted at his passing with a mixture of respect, fear, and dread.

From that day forward, Stres was never seen again. No one, neither his deputies nor his family, not even his wife, knew where he was—or at least no one would say.

At the Old Monastery the wooden grandstands and platform were dismantled, workmen carried off the planks and beams, and in the inner courtyard there was no longer any trace of the assembly. But no one forgot a word that Stres had spoken there. His words passed from mouth to mouth, from village to village, with unbelievable speed. The rumor that Stres had been arrested in the wake of his speech soon proved unfounded. It was said that he had been seen somewhere, or at least that someone had heard the trot of his horse. Others insisted they had caught a glimpse of him on the northern highway. They were sure they had recognized him, despite the dusk and the first layer of dust that covered his hair. Who can say? people mused, who can say? How much, O Lord, must our poor minds take in! And then someone said, his voice trembling as if shivering with cold:

"Sometimes I wonder if he didn't bring Doruntine back himself."

"How dare you say such a thing?"

"What would be so surprising?" the man answered. "As for myself, I have not been surprised by anything since the day she returned."

During this time people began to talk more than ever of the harm caused by far-off marriages. Though no one would admit it, everyone felt a vague nostalgia for local marriages, an echo of an even more secret longing—for marriages within the clan itself. Those days were gone, but people missed them. Was it not repentance that had raised Constantine from his grave?

That's what people said. And it was just then that something happened which would have seemed only too natural at any other time: a young village bride set off to join her husband in a far-off land. Everyone was astounded to hear of this new Doruntine at a time when it was thought that the very idea of distant marriages had suffered its *coup de grâce*. After everything that had just happened, it was expected that the bride's family would break the engagement, or at least postpone the marriage. But no. The wedding took place on the scheduled date, the groom's relatives arrived from their country, which some said lay six days distant, others eight, and after much eating, drinking, and song, they led the young bride away. Nearly all the village accompanied her from the church, as once they had walked with the unfortunate Doruntine, and as they gazed upon the young bride so beautiful and misty in her white veil, there were many who must have wondered whether a ghost would carry her home some moonless night. But she, mounted on a white horse, showed not the slightest apprehension about her fate. And the people, following her with their eyes, shook their heads and said, "Good God, maybe young brides today like this sort of thing. Perhaps they like to ride by night, clasping a shadow, through the gloom and the void. . . ."

Tirana, October 1979